# Forlorn Hope
## The Storming of Badajoz

A novella by
# James Mace

D1366321

Legionary Books
Meridian, Idaho 83642, USA
http://www.legionarybooks.net

First eBook Edition: 2012

Published in the United States of America
Legionary Books
http://www.legionarybooks.net

# The Works of James Mace

**The Artorian Chronicles**
Soldier of Rome: The Legionary (Book One)
Soldier of Rome: The Sacrovir Revolt (Book Two)
Soldier of Rome: Heir to Rebellion (Book Three)
Soldier of Rome: The Centurion (Book Four)
Soldier of Rome: Journey to Judea (Book Five)
Soldier of Rome: The Last Campaign (Book Six)

**Other Works**
I Stood With Wellington
Forlorn Hope: The Storming of Badajoz
Centurion Valens and the Empress of Death
Empire Betrayed: The Fall of Sejanus

*The hardest thing of all for a soldier to do is retreat.*

- Arthur Wellesley, 1<sup>st</sup> Duke of Wellington

# Preface

In the spring of 1812, the British army under Sir Arthur Wellesley, Earl of Wellington, has driven the French from Portugal. With Napoleon obsessed by the invasion of Russia, Wellington turns toward Spain. The way is barred by two fortresses, Ciudad Rodrigo and Badajoz. When Ciudad Rodrigo collapses after a short siege, Wellington prepares to break the fortress of Badajoz, the most formidable stronghold in Europe and commanded by the seasoned warrior, Baron Armand Philippon. Despite a shortage of engineers and equipment, Wellington must seize Badajoz if he is to have any chance of driving into Spain. When he learns that an army under Marshal Soult is en route to relieve Badajoz, Wellington risks being caught between Soult and Philippon and must execute the attack on Badajoz immediately. If he fails, the British will be trapped between two armies and lose everything for which they and their allies have fought for the past four years.

Lieutenant James Webster is in mourning following the loss of his wife, and he volunteers to command the small group that will lead the assault. Second in command is Sergeant Thomas Davis; recently diagnosed with a fatal illness, he prefers a valiant death in battle. Breaches have been blown into the walls of the southern bastions, Trinidad and Santa Maria, and here Wellington will unleash the 4th and Light Divisions, while launching diversionary assaults on the northern San Vincente bastion, as well as the Badajoz castle. Together with one hundred volunteers, the *Forlorn Hope,* Webster and Davis will storm into the breach.

## Cast of Characters
### Soldier of the Forlorn Hope:

**Lieutenant James Webster** – Volunteers to lead the Forlorn Hope into the Trinidad bastion

**Lieutenant Benedict Harvest** – Friend of Lieutenant Webster, he is leading the Light Division's Forlorn Hope into the Santa Maria bastion

**Sergeant Thomas Davis** – Senior-ranking non-commissioned officer, acts as Webster's second

**Corporals Patrick Shanahan, Frederick Sharp** – Non-commissioned officers

**Privates William Lawrence, John Reynolds** – Enlisted men

### British Commanders:

**Arthur Wellesley, Earl of Wellington**[1] – Commander in Chief

**Major General Thomas Picton** – Commander of the 3rd Division that led the attack on the Badajoz Castle

**Major General Lowry Cole** – Commander of the 4th Division that attacked the breach at La Trinidad bastion

**Major General James Leith** – Commander of the 5th Division that attacked the San Vincente bastion

### The French:

**Armand Philippon** – Governor of Badajoz

**Gerard Aubert** – A colonel serving under Philippon, responsible for defending the Trinidad bastion

[1] Note: Wellington was not made a Duke until May 1814

# Prologue
## Badajoz, Spain
### March 1812

It was a hateful task for a British infantryman. The tools of his trade were the musket and bayonet, not the shovel and pickaxe! Yet, despite the protestations of their commander-in-chief, Arthur Wellesley, Earl of Wellington, they were deprived of sufficient engineers and siege equipment. Wellington's complaints to London after the assault on Ciudad Rodrigo had fallen, mostly, on deaf ears. Now he was faced with taking the most formidable fortress in all of Europe, without so much as a practical siege train. Thus did the majority of the entrenching fall upon the infantryman, of which there was no short supply. In all, twenty-seven thousand redcoats surrounded the impenetrable fortress.

The late winter rains had been relentless, and the ground around the city of Badajoz was a drenched mass of mud and clay. The conditions for the besieging army were terrible. The constant rain left them perpetually soaked and freezing, leading to many an illness amongst the ranks. The sodden ground made transportation of the logistics trains extremely difficult, and every soldier felt as if he had several pounds of clay perpetually stuck to his boots. Possibly the only good thing to come from the otherwise deplorable conditions, was that the work crews on the trench lines did not make the same racket they had on the dry and rocky ground around Ciudad Rodrigo. Instead, the tools made hardly a sound as they sunk into the earth, though it seemed for every shovel full of mud a soldier dug up, he'd spend an additional minute scraping the caked-on clay from his tool.

On this particular day, the rain was mercifully not falling, although the sky was shrouded in black clouds, and the wind blew cold. The commanding officer in charge of one section of the line seemed oblivious to the activity going on across the open field towards the enemy lines. The British army had been attempting to entrench around Badajoz, and knowing that they were short on engineer tools, the French commander, Baron Philippon, had promised a reward to any defender who brought back a shovel or

9

entrenching tool. As such, the French were audaciously launching an assault on a portion of the siege lines in order to secure their tools.

*"Here they come!"*

Hundreds of French soldiers raced across the open ground, knowing they'd caught the British off guard. Only a single officer from the 88th Regiment, known as the Connaught Rangers, had taken the liberty to post sentries to watch for such an incursion.

*"Fall in on your weapons!"* this officer shouted to his men.

Sporadic shots rang out from the charging French; musket balls slapping into the mud with a dull thud. As Colonel Fletcher, the British chief engineer, rode up on his horse to see what the commotion was, he was struck down by a musket shot and fell hard to the earth, groaning in pain.

"The colonel's down!" a soldier called out.

The men, caught by complete surprise, quickly decided between falling back the one hundred yards to where their weapons were stacked or attempting to fight the French off with their shovels and pickaxes. Within seconds the decision was made for them, as the enemy fell upon them with musket and bayonet. As French infantrymen attacked the near-helpless entrenchers, their comrades started picking up scores of shovels and pickaxes. Though the British who remained in the trenches fought on bravely, shovels were unwieldy against a musket with a long bayonet fixed. As companies of infantry fell on their weapons and rushed back into the fray, they formed up and fired the occasional volley of musket fire, which started to pick off the French attackers. Having accomplished what they set out to do, a French officer shouted for his men to retire. Though each side suffered approximately a hundred casualties in the skirmish, it was a terrible blow for the British. The French fell back towards Badajoz, laughing amongst themselves at having made off with an entire section's worth of entrenching tools.

Despite the volume of fire coming from French troops set to cover the retreat of the raiders, one very young British lieutenant calmly climbed onto the berm, pistol in hand. Bullets slapped the ground around him as he casually levelled his weapon at the retreating French officer and fired. It should have been nothing more than a parting shot, as the French were now well beyond the pitiful range of a flintlock pistol. Yet, inexplicably, the back of the French officer's head exploded in a spray of pink mist and grey matter. His twitching corpse fell onto its stomach and slid a few feet across the saturated earth. Despite the magnitude of the disaster, a loud cheer rang up from the British ranks as the young officer strolled down the embankment, his face serenely calm.

On the French side of the lines there was a raucous cheer as hundreds of raiders rushed into the city, bearing shovels, pickaxes, and other entrenching tools. Though it had cost them scores of dead and even more wounded, who were now prisoners of the British, they had deprived an entire section of their much-needed equipment, exacerbating their already hateful task. However, a colonel who stood on the ramparts over-watching the skirmish was not cheering his men's success. His gaze was fixed upon the young officer who had led the raid and now lay facedown in the muck, his brains splattered from the smash of the pistol shot. The colonel took a deep breath through his nose and fought back the single tear that ran down his face.

# Chapter I: Someone Has to Go First
Badajoz, Spain
5 April 1812

Sir Arthur Wellesley, Earl (later Duke) of Wellington

*"Someone has to go first."*

*This was my official explanation to the colonel when he asked me why in God's name I would submit my name for the Forlorn Hope. Early this morning, I was selected by lottery to lead the one hundred volunteers of the 4th Division that will attempt to gain a foothold in the Trinidad bastion before the first wave attacks. Though numerous officers submitted their names, the colonel said he always felt I had more sense than to ask for an assignment that almost certainly means death or serious injury. He was particularly befuddled that I put in my request the day before the assault.*

*It was only after much prodding, not to mention threats of reprimand, that I confessed my actual reasons for volunteering. The colonel immediately became supportive of my decision and agreed that someone does have to go first. The difficulty now will be explaining myself to Daniel; who though my captain, has been more of a friend than a commanding officer over the last three years. In a sign of true friendship, I suspect he will shed the tears I cannot when I tell him the news regarding my beloved Amy.*

*Our cannon have successfully blown two breaches and I will lead the Forlorn Hope into the one called Trinidad. I heard that young Lieutenant Harvest was selected to go into the Santa Maria breach; a good career move, provided we both live. And if not, God willing, I will be with Amy again.*

*Tonight or the next day death will come in all its beautiful brutality.*

*Lieutenant James Henry Webster*
*5 April 1812*

The deafening thunder of cannon startled the young officer out of his thoughts.

"I thought they said the breach was practicable," he grunted to himself. "Why the devil are they still firing?" As much as the heavy siege guns had been firing over the previous two weeks, it was a wonder that their crews weren't completely deaf. In all, twenty thousand heavy cannonballs had been launched into the stubborn walls of the city. Just getting the siege guns and ammunition to Badajoz had been a feat of logistics. Wellington had ordered thousands of Portuguese militiamen to each carry a single twenty-four pound cannonball in his pack. Though there had been much grumbling over this, it saved on having to procure additional wagons, plus it left Wellington's British troops available to fight.

The young officer stepped out of his tent and into the afternoon sun. Though the light blinded him for a moment, he was grateful to finally see the sun once more. For weeks it had been pouring rain on the besiegers of Badajoz. The ground was still saturated, the grass downtrodden by the rain and the footfalls of thousands of men and horses, and turned into a mire of mud and detritus. Frowning, he looked down on his highly polished boots and thought of what they would look like by the end of the day. The young man threw on his red frock coat, with its single epaulette denoting his rank as a lieutenant.

His name was James Henry Webster. Twenty-four years of age, he had served as an officer in Wellington's army since the landing in Portugal, nearly four years prior. The youngest of six sons, he had few prospects in life, despite his family's wealth. Oddly enough, none of his older brothers wore the King's uniform. So when James expressed a desire to serve with the expeditionary force being sent to Portugal, his father had been enthusiastic in helping him attain his commission. Insisting that his son would only serve in the best regiments, his father had purchased his commission into the 1st Foot Guards and sent him on his way, 'To either die for King George or to live in the glory of victory'.

Despite his father's protestations, James had married his childhood love, Amy, soon after his commissioning. They had but three weeks together before his regiment was sent to Portugal with Wellington, who at the time was simply Lieutenant General Arthur Wellesley.

During the early days in Portugal, James had served as one of two lieutenants within his company; the other being a young man named Daniel Roberts, who was a few years older than James and from a far more influential family. When their captain was killed at Talavera almost four years before, Daniel was promoted into the position. The young officer who acquired his lieutenancy lost a leg at Fuentes de Onoro the previous May and since then had not been replaced. In addition to the officers, a company had over one hundred other ranks, including five non-commissioned officers consisting of two sergeants and three corporals. As companies within the Foot Guards were often larger than in other units, Captain Daniels had received permission to promote two additional privates to corporal.

Eight line companies, each commanded by a captain, made up a battalion, with an additional company of grenadiers, as well as a light company of skirmishers. The battalion was commanded by a lieutenant colonel, along with two majors. The majors would each take command of a 'wing' consisting of several companies during battle, taking their orders from the lieutenant colonel. The number of battalions within a regiment varied considerably. Many regiments consisted of a single battalion; others, such as the 88th Foot, also known as the Connaught Rangers, had two battalions. Conversely, the enormous 60th Foot had seven battalions, one of which was entirely made up of elite riflemen who wore green jackets instead of red and carried Baker rifles instead of muskets. James' own regiment of the 1st Foot Guards consisted of three battalions.

Amy had insisted on accompanying James, as she felt it was her duty to see to his needs. Officers were allowed to bring their wives, provided their commanding officers approved. As neither Daniel Roberts nor their previous captain had been married, Amy was the only officer's wife within the company, though there were others within the battalion. Up to six wives of the other ranks from each company were authorized to join their husbands on campaign. They were placed on the company roles, given a half-share of rations, and also subject to the same camp discipline as their spouses. This dispensation of allowing wives on campaign had little to do with compassion, but was a matter of practicality. Spouses of the rankers would provide laundry, mending of uniforms, as well as care for the sick and wounded. As a significant number of the men were married, selection for those carried on the company roles was done by lottery. Wives not selected were still permitted to travel with their husbands. However, they were not authorized a ration and, therefore, had to be cared for at their own expense.

Despite her lack of years and having lived a privileged existence, Amy endured the hardships of campaign with much dignity and perseverance. The wives of the other ranks adored her, despite the vast difference in class. Though she was younger than most, her education and social status made her a type of mother figure amongst the company wives. She even went as far as to help those who were pregnant when it came time to give birth. The British army understood that by allowing wives on campaign, children had to be accounted for as well. A child born to a British soldier whose wife was on the roles was authorized a quarter rations per day.

While childbirth was not uncommon on campaign, it was still very arduous, with mother and child sometimes succumbing. So when it was discovered that Amy was with child, James had compiled all his money together to buy her transport back to England. He did not wish for his wife to endure the inherent risks that came from carrying and then delivering a child in the Spanish wilderness. A few of his friends had loaned him money to help Amy return home, including Lieutenant Harvest. That was eight months

15

ago, and Amy had been at least six weeks along when she left. James had heard no word from her and was deeply concerned.

Early on the morning of 4 April, James finally received word from home. The letter was not from his wife, like he'd hoped, but rather from his sister, Angela. In the brief span that it took to read the short letter, his entire life came crashing down.

*Dearest Brother,*

*It is with a mixture of both joy and terrible sadness that I write to you. Amy had a very hard confinement and the last few days sapped most of her strength. She bore you a beautiful baby girl, but regrettably succumbed to complications and died soon after. Your daughter is doing well. Since you had left no guidance on a name, I decided to call her Amy, after her mother. Father said you would approve. My heart breaks at the loss of your wife, but take comfort in knowing that she is with God and your daughter is well loved. She will be waiting for you, as we all will.*

*Your loving sister,*
*Angela*

The letter was dated a month prior and did not say exactly when James' daughter was born or when he lost his wife. It was incomprehensible to him, being a father. He had never seen his daughter, and she was unknowable to him. And now that he had been selected for the Forlorn Hope, most likely he would never see her. He was still in shock over the news and hoped he would be spared from the pending despair until the assault. He reasoned that he had not broken down in tears, perhaps, because he would most likely be dead himself and therefore reunited with his love. It would be a tragedy for his daughter to lose both her parents, but he took solace in the knowledge that his family would care for her. It was difficult to give her any real thought or emotion, as she did not even seem real to him.

*"Lieutenant Webster!"* The shout of his commanding officer caught his attention and gave him a much-needed distraction.

James turned and saluted. "Yes, sir."

Captain Daniel Roberts ignored it, his face flush with worry. "I heard you were selected for the Forlorn Hope."

He then knew why Daniel was vexed. The two were close in age and over the last four years had become firm friends. They had fought together at Vimeiro and Talavera, where Daniel was promoted to captain. Both knew the pending assault on Badajoz would be terrible; far worse than what they had seen at Ciudad Rodrigo, less than four months prior.

"Damn it, man," Daniel cursed, shaking his head. "I heard Benedict Harvest drew the other breach. You know you've all gone completely mad."

"It is a great risk," James conceded, "but a momentous opportunity. We are but a few years apart in age, and yet my career prospects are few. You have patronage and money. I have barely enough to hold on to my commission. Unless I do something heroic or somehow gain a patron, I daresay I will still be languishing as a lieutenant when you're a colonel. By leading the Forlorn Hope into Badajoz, I, too, may be given a company command."

"That's not the only reason," Daniel said solemnly.

James' face twitched. "You heard about Amy. How? I have not told anyone."

"John Cooke had gone to see you," Daniel explained. "He was about to enter your tent when he heard you talking. He thought there was somebody in there with you, but then remembered that you tend to read your letters aloud. I am sorry for your loss." He put a comforting hand on his James' shoulder. There was already the trace of a tear in his eye; the ones he would shed that his friend could not.

"I do not blame you for volunteering for the Forlorn Hope," the captain continued. "I know more than a dozen officers threw their names into the lot."

"Many reasoned that we're all dead anyway," James observed. "So we may as well take a chance at glory; or in the least, expedite our inevitable demise. You know we all stand a significant chance of falling."

"I know," Daniel conceded. "But at least when I go in, I will have the entire regiment with over four thousand men with me. The Forlorn Hope has but a hundred. Your only mission is to get a foothold into the breach and pray you're not already dead when the

17

first wave assaults. And as an officer, every frog gunner is going to be aiming for your head."

Casualties amongst officers on both sides were always exceedingly high. Differing hats and stark contrasts in uniforms drew a disproportionate amount of enemy fire to the officers. It was for this reason many elected to forgo their traditional bicorn hats in favour of the stovepipe shakos worn by the other ranks. James had elected to keep his bicorn, figuring he should look the part of a proper officer, if and when he should fall.

"Well," James reasoned, "if they're all aiming for my head, at least I'll die quickly."

"I'll miss you, James," Daniel said, ignoring his subaltern's dark humour. "Many of the lads were both proud and saddened to hear you were selected."

"Why would they be saddened?" James asked.

"You've been a good officer to them," the captain answered. "You've got just enough education and class to be a proper officer, without being a total aristocratic snob like Old Nosey."

James chuckled at the nickname the men used for Wellington, given his prominent nose. Wellington was very much aware of the name, though far from being offended, he found the moniker flattering. The rankers had a number of names for him, and he for them; none of which were remotely affectionate. This was a sharp contrast to one of Wellington's most dependable generals, Sir Rowland Hill, whose men called him 'daddy'.

"A snob he may be," James replied, "But he's an effective snob."

The commander-in-chief was a difficult man to like. He was short with his officers and disdainful towards the men in the ranks. Though while the army bore no love for him, like they did for 'Daddy' Hill, what he did have was their undying respect. Thus far, he had been the only commanding general in all of Europe that proved able to stand up to Napoleon's unstoppable juggernaut. He had taken a ragtag army, brought up from the very dregs of society, and turned them into a highly-skilled and iron-disciplined fighting force. He had also given them something that had been denied every major army that dared to stand against Napoleon, and that was victory. Since landing in Portugal and engaging the French at the first major battles of the campaign at Rolica and Vimeiro, Wellington had decisively defeated Napoleon's best generals time and again, with troops who were far less experienced and almost always outnumbered. He had done the unthinkable and driven the French for Portugal, yet for whatever reason, Napoleon largely continued to ignore him. Perhaps he reckoned that despite the efforts of Spanish insurrectionists to tie up the French army, once Wellington did get into Spain, he'd be horribly outnumbered and easily swept aside. Or maybe he simply assumed that the British and their allies would never be able to break the French hold on Badajoz and, thereby, never even make it into Spain.

# Chapter II: Soult's Return
## Wellington's Headquarters
## 10:00 a.m.

Marshal Nicolas Soult, Duke of Dalmatia

"Your grace, I beg of you," Alten pleaded, "give us a week...even just a few more days for the artillery to weaken the defences!" The commander of the Light Division, Major General Charles Alten, feared that despite there being two sizeable breaches in the walls of Badajoz, they were still too well defended for his men to effectively assault. He had recently been given command of the division; its previous commander, the renowned General Robert Craufurd, having been killed at Ciudad Rodrigo. Alten was a capable enough officer, though he was certainly no Craufurd.

For all his flaws, and despite many heated arguments they had had, Wellington was feeling Craufurd's loss as they prepared to storm Badajoz. "The artillery has had two weeks. And I have personally checked our chief engineer's assessment that the breaches are now practicable." As was typical of the commander-in-chief, he personally observed the work the artillery had done in breaching the

Trinidad and Santa Maria bastions. Wellington's one admitted weakness was the lack of trust in the judgment of his subordinates, and so he had to check for himself rather than rely solely on the engineer's perspective. Such 'lead-from-the-front' style of command had almost cost him his life on more than one occasion, and this day was no different; as Wellington knew, in order to get a close enough view of the breaches, he would have to place himself well within range of the French batteries in both the Trinidad and Santa Maria bastions.

"Colonel Fletcher," Wellington continued, turning to his engineer chief, "you have also assured me the breaches are practicable."

"Yes, sir," Fletcher replied. His arm was in a sling, and his face pale. He was still feeling the effects of his injuries from the skirmish with the French raiders that had seen him shot off his horse. "I will say, though, that while the breaches are large enough, they are very well-defended. They can still provide overlapping cannon and musket fire. We simply do not have the necessary heavy guns to destroy the bastions and their gun emplacements."

It was not just his assessment of the breaches that led Wellington to his decision to launch the assault sooner rather than later. To emphasize his reasons, he produced a map of the region. Positions of the British forces and a handful of Portuguese allies were marked around Badajoz.

"If it were up to me, I would give you all the time you needed to smash the frogs into oblivion before attacking," Wellington explained. "However, as in any battle, the enemy has a say in our plans as well. It may interest you to know that Marshal Soult is en route to relieve the garrison with an army of thirty thousand men. Between his forces and Baron Philippon's army within Badajoz, they will have us in a bad position if we are caught between them. We must strike now!"

The assembled leaders then gathered around a large diagram of the City of Badajoz. Though the 4th and Light Divisions under Alten and Sir Galbraith Lowry Cole would have the most hazardous mission with going into the breaches, the other two prongs of the attack were also incredibly perilous. To the northeast, where the formidable castle stood, were marked the avenues of approach for Thomas Picton's 3rd Division. To the northwest, along the San

Vincente bastion, Sir James Leith would assault with his 5$^{th}$ Division.

"We cannot have every defender massed on the breaches, otherwise we'll never get in," Wellington explained. "Therefore, Picton and Leith will launch simultaneous secondary assaults on the castle and San Vincente bastions."

"Secondary," Picton scoffed.

Wellington glared at him. "Do you find your assignment distasteful, General Picton?"

"Only in its implication that we are not supposed to succeed," Picton remarked. "I will wager not only will the *Fighting 3$^{rd}$* take the castle, but we will be the first into Badajoz."

"I'll take that wager," Leith replied. "The 5$^{th}$ Division will take the San Vincente bastion, even without a practicable breach!"

Though Wellington personally felt the two men's assertions to be little more than peacock strutting, he appreciated their eagerness and knew such attitudes would pass on to their men. Still, he knew the best chance for overcoming such a formidable obstacle, which had withstood two previous sieges, would fall on the shoulders of the 4$^{th}$ and Light Divisions. And while Alten was no Robert Craufurd, his men were still the same hardened bastards who'd fought so well taking Ciudad Rodrigo. Here was a chance for Alten to prove himself worthy of taking the Division as his own.

"General Lowry Cole," Wellington said, addressing the other division commander, "any apprehensions about taking the Trinidad bastion?"

"Plenty, your grace," Lowry Cole replied candidly. "The deep trench may be flooded, and the area is doubtless chock full of mines and other traps; all in an area so compacted that a blind man could shoot at us and score a hit each time. However, the 4$^{th}$ Division has a knack for achieving the impossible."

Major General Sir Galbraith Lowry Cole was a former member of the House of Commons and a battle-tested field commander. He had served with distinction at the Battle of Maida in 1806; one of the few early successes against the French Empire. More recently, the previous May, he'd played a decisive role in the Battle of Albuera where he was wounded. Wellington surmised that his promotion to lieutenant general was simply a matter of time, provided he didn't get himself killed. Like Picton, he was known for leading from the front, and while this garnered much respect from the ranks, it was a leadership style that had cost Robert Craufurd his life.

Though Ciudad Rodrigo seemed like an arduous siege at the time, it had fallen relatively quickly, with the defenders, surprisingly, suffering greater losses than the exposed attackers. Wellington knew, with its thirty-foot walls, in some places fifteen feet thick, coupled with bastions that provided interlocking fields of cannon and musket fire, all surrounded by a steep trench, Badajoz would prove far more difficult, if not impossible, to break.

The hundred men who would make up the 4th Division's Forlorn Hope stood in formation. They were a makeshift conglomeration of men from various regiments, noted by the subtle and sometimes not-so-subtle differences in their uniforms. Though most wore the traditional redcoats with various coloured facings to denote their individual regiments, there were half-a-dozen men sporting the green jackets similar to those worn by the 95th Rifles. The sergeant, who stood in front of the formation, wore a green jacket with red facings that denoted the 5th Battalion of the 60th Foot. Though their weaponry and tactics were similar to the more famous 95th, they were part of a much larger line regiment and acted as their skirmishers. Privately, James was glad to see a handful of green jackets, as riflemen were known for their ability to act independently in the absence of orders. In the chaos that was certain to ensue during the pending assault, this would prove invaluable, provided any of them survived long enough to make it into the breach.

"Forlorn Hope assembled, sir," the sergeant said, snapping off a sharp salute which James returned.

"And you are?" he asked.

"Sergeant Thomas Davis, 5th Battalion, 60th Regiment, sir!" Upon his last word, the sergeant broke into a fearful coughing fit.

James took a step back and stood for a moment with his eyebrows raised.

When the man had finished, his face was red, with a tear rolling down each cheek. "Apologies, sir."

"Carry on, sergeant," James replied. He then shouted to the men, "Stand at ease!"

There were only two other non-commissioned officers besides Sergeant Davis; both corporals. As James knew that they would be the ones to lead the Forlorn whenever he should fall, he'd best get to know a little about them in the few hours they had before the attack.

"Name?" he said, walking over to the first.

"Corporal Patrick Shanahan, 27th Regiment, sir!" the man snapped with a heavily accented Irish brogue.

James acknowledged him and walked over to the other man.

"And you?"

"Corporal Frederick Sharp, 40th Regiment, sir!"

James nodded and then faced the formation.

*"Gentlemen,"* he shouted, with a prominent command voice that contrasted sharply with his boyish appearance. *My name is Lieutenant Webster. Some of you may have volunteered hoping for a chance at fame and glory, as we will be first into the breach. We are here for one purpose, to hold the Trinidad bastion and most likely die in place, so get any notions you may have of glory out of your minds! A few may survive unscathed, but for the rest of us, if God has any mercy, He will grant us a quick death."*

"Sir, a number of us were at Ciudad Rodrigo," Sergeant Davis replied calmly. "We know what you're asking for."

"King George commands and we obey," Corporal Shanahan added.

"Very good," James remarked. He then addressed the men once more. *"Arms inspection will be at 1700 hours. Until then, you are free to spend the day getting your affairs in order and making ready for the assault. That is all."* He then nodded to Sergeant Davis, who saluted and turned to face the assembly.

*"Company!"* he shouted. *"Attention...dismissed!"* He immediately fell into another coughing fit as the men of the Forlorn Hope dispersed.

James was slowly walking away, hands clasped behind his back, as Sergeant Davis rushed up to him.

"Lieutenant Webster!" he called, trying to stifle his coughing once more.

James turned and faced him as the sergeant spoke again.

"Apologies again."

24

"Does your cough have anything to do with why you are here?" the Lieutenant asked.

"Aye, it does, sir," Davis replied, embarrassed. "Started happening even before Ciudad Rodrigo. Two weeks ago, I was finally diagnosed. The doctors say I'll live maybe another year before the good Lord takes me. The colonel offered to send me home, but I'd have none of it. I said the goodbyes to me wife and sons before we left for Portugal. I'd rather they pretended I died valiantly, rather than watching a sick man waste away in their sight."

"And supposing you survive?" James asked.

Sergeant Davis chuckled and shook his head. "I won't, sir. I'll see if I can stay alive long enough for us to get a hold on the breach. After that, I'll walk straight into a frog cannon if I have to."

"I'm glad to have you, sergeant," James remarked. "You won't balk when it gets bloody."

"And you, sir," the sergeant replied. "You're a smart-looking officer; good command voice, too. That helps inspire the lads. Something about knowing that even the most proper officers and gentlemen are willing to die with them makes the men more willing to throw themselves straight into oblivion."

James smiled and the two men walked in silence together. He didn't know where he was going. He simply felt like walking. Since Sergeant Davis would be his second going into the breach, and given the likelihood they would fall together, he was glad for the man's company. Cannon continued to thunder, breaking greater gaps into the breaches while tormenting the French defenders inside. Though the ground was still sodden, the rain had ceased, and the sun felt warm in their faces. Looking down he noticed the mud was drying on his boots.

"Must get my man to shine them again," he thought aloud, "Can't very well die looking slovenly."

"Do you have any children, sir?" Davis asked after a few minutes.

James stopped in his tracks.

The sergeant's expression grew uncomfortable. "I don't mean to intrude, sir. I just saw your wedding ring and thought I'd ask."

"Not at all," James replied as they continued walking. "I have a daughter. Her name is Amy."

"Ah, beautiful lass, I bet," Davis replied, smiling once more. Doubtless taken back to memories of his own children that he had not seen in nearly four years.

"Well if she takes after her mother," James answered with a short laugh. "To be honest, I wouldn't know. I've never seen her."

"Pity that," Davis observed. "I, at least, had a full life with me sons. Sad though I am that I'll never see them again, I still thank God for the time He gave me with them. What then of your wife, sir?"

James' countenance darkened.

"She died, soon after giving birth to our daughter," he answered. "She accompanied me all through Portugal. When we found she was with child I sent her home, for her well-being and that of our daughter's. I only received word yesterday that I lost her."

"My deepest condolences for your loss. If I may pry again, sir, is that why you are here?"

"It is," James acknowledged. "For an officer there is, of course, great chance for glory and career advancement. Hence, many of my fellows, lacking in patronage, volunteered in droves to lead the Forlorn. I added my name just yesterday, after hearing news of my wife."

"And you wish to be with her again," Davis added. "Sir, if I may be so bold; whatever happens to us rankers, an officer who leads the Forlorn Hope and survives becomes a hero. His career is set, regardless of past patronage. Hell, potential patrons will come seeking *him* out! I daresay, sir, if you live to see the morrow, you will be *Captain* Webster. A captain in the King's army, especially one whose reputation will echo across the globe, will have much to offer his child. Should you make it through this, sir, *live*…if not for yourself, for your daughter's sake."

The sergeant's words struck close to home for the young officer. Davis didn't know he was already regretting his decision to volunteer for the Forlorn and, unlike the sergeant, he would not be walking into a French cannon if he could avoid it. The idea of making captain had an undeniable appeal to it. As it was, his lack of funds and patronage meant he'd have to be satisfied serving as a lieutenant for the foreseeable future. He'd most likely not see captain until he was in his thirties. Whereas leading the Forlorn Hope and surviving would ensure that, by the same age, he'd most likely be a major or perhaps even a lieutenant colonel with command of a battalion. Such prospects boded well, not just for himself, but for little Amy. She would be far better off having an established officer for a father than growing up an orphan, living with her unwed aunt.

The very fact that he was even discussing such personal matters with a soldier from the ranks was, in itself, an anomaly that broke the norms of social etiquette. Enlisted men took orders from their officers and executed them, nothing more. An occasional *"good day"* would be the extent of pleasantries between them. James had gotten to know a few of the men in his company, mainly because of their similarity in age; the average age of a British soldier from the ranks being approximately twenty-three. Despite this, interaction was still very limited and almost always formal. In the 95th Rifles, as well as Davis' own battalion of the 60th Regiment, protocols were different. Out of necessity, officers messed and bivouacked with their men. They were used to working in small groups and, unlike their counterparts in the line companies, riflemen were encouraged to think for themselves and make quick decisions on their own. An officer in the rifles who wished to foster creative thinking had to get to know his men on a more personal level than an officer on a battle line, who had only to teach his men to fire quickly and exercise extreme bravery when the order to charge was given. As a non-commissioned officer within a rifle company, Sergeant Davis no doubt had to be far more candid with his officers than was normally expected. James pointed this out.

"I got on well with my officers, yes," Davis conceded. "Not to worry, sir, their living so closely with us rankers does not diminish their status as proper officers and gentlemen."

"Having an understanding of one's men is never a bad thing," James replied.

"No, sir, of course not," Davis said. He then paused before continuing, *"Scum of the earth* is what Wellington calls us. Well, I daresay it's not without good reason."

"And it doesn't offend you?" James asked.

Sergeant Davis shook his head and gave a knowing grin. "As I was saying, sir, it is not without reason that Old Nosey refers to us with such disdain. You, sir, were raised with a proper education, learned to read and write as soon as you learned to walk, that sort of thing. You were already well-schooled before you ever donned the King's uniform. As for me, I joined the ranks much in the same

27

manner as many of the lads. Most join because we have no other options in life, lest we wish to starve to death in the gutters. The recruiting sergeant popped into the local ale house at a time when he knew most of us would be piss-drunk. I had just lost me job working in the fields that very morning, so I was good and buggered up by the time the man with the nice red uniform popped in. Held aloft a King's shilling, did he. Chatted us up about service to King George, though I can't reckon a word of what he said. It was a bleeding mess when I returned home to tell me wife that not only had I lost my job, but I joined the bloody army!"

"A small wonder then, that we issue each lad a half cup of gin before going into battle," James observed.

"I quit drinking right after taking the King's shilling," Davis replied, "though a cup or two might set me straight before I have my meeting with the Almighty this evening."

James marvelled at the vast differences between himself and the sergeant, who was so freely sharing his last hours alive with him. That they were both Englishmen was about the only similarity they shared. Despite what he felt were poor career prospects, Davis was right; he did have a decent education, had never had to worry about living on the streets growing up, and starvation was unknown to him. The cost of his humble lieutenant's commission was still more money than most rankers had ever seen. Even non-commissioned officers made scarcely more than a private; something that irked Wellington to no end. While he and his officers dictated policy, it was the sergeants and their corporals who had to enforce it on their mates. A sergeant with a family, like Thomas Davis, had far less disposable income than a bachelor private. It was because of this Wellington had persistently harangued Horse Guards and London about better wages for the non-commissioned officers. If a corporal or sergeant was expected to put his men to the lash, then he needed to be compensated for it.

In a world of rigid social class, the army was a melding of societies. The aristocracy provided the officers, while the other ranks came from the poor classes. Probably the most difficult position within the army was the extremely rare case of a former-enlisted officer. His peers would shun him, and even the men he led would look upon him with disdain, often saying, 'You're not a proper officer, you're still one of us, *sir*.' And yet for all that, all stood

28

together in battle; men who came from completely different worlds were willing to die together.

The hammering of the British guns had become numbing for Gerard and the other defenders of Badajoz. The people living in the city were completely trapped. Though most hated living under the iron fist of Bonaparte's rule, there was also a lot of apprehension as to what would happen to them should the British succeed in taking the stronghold. It had not taken long for the stories of abject cruelty inflicted upon the populace of Ciudad Rodrigo to reach them. The women, especially, were terrified at the prospect of being mistreated by enraged redcoats, whose vengeance would undoubtably be fueled by drink and beastly lust.

Gerard Aubert was in his early forties and a highly-experienced colonel. He had been a major at Austerlitz seven years prior, in what was often viewed as Napoleon's greatest victory. The combined Russian and Austrian armies had been destroyed, their losses ten times that of the French. It cemented the notion of French invincibility on land, and helped ease the scourge brought on by the destruction of their navy by the British at Trafalgar just prior. And yet, despite the power of their navy, in 1805 the British did not have a land army that could be thought of as even a remote threat to the unstoppable Bonaparte. The British were confined to their island and remote colonial posessions, while Napoleon became master of Europe.

Yet, for all his experience, Gerard's knowledge paled when compared to his commander's. Baron Armand Philippon had worn the French uniform for more than thirty years, having started in the ranks as a private and rising all the way to sergeant major before commissioning. Unlike the British, the French military culture encouraged officers who came up from the ranks. Another contrast between the two was the men in the ranks. France utilized conscription, while the British army was all-volunteer. This meant that the French army was composed of a greater swath of the social classes, while the British, officers aside, was made up of those who enlisted because they had no other skills or job prospects. One decisive advantage the British did have was in training of its troops. Due to the almost continuous warfare on the continent, French conscripts were often sent into battle with only the most rudimentary training in musketry and tactics. Due to their isolation and immense national wealth, the British were able to spend months training their soldiers, making them, more often, better-drilled and superior marksmen.

Armand Philippon had been personally trained by Napoleon, and the French emperor trusted him completely to hold onto Badajoz. So great was his trust, he was proceeding with his planned invasion of Russia, rather than devoting the majority of his resources to defeating this British upstart who'd tossed his army out of Portugal. As long as Badajoz held, Wellington was unable to advance into Spain, and Napoleon figured it would only be a matter of time before his armies were able to converge upon and destroy him.

"We may have the walls to protect us," Gerard observed, turning to Philippon. "But Wellington now has the advantage in numbers."

"I'd say he has us bested more than five-to-one," Philippon agreed, eyeing the British heavy siege guns through his telescope.

They both stood atop the highest tower of the castle, where they could see Wellington's entire army surrounding them. It was, indeed, an impressive, albeit terrifying sight.

"Still, I would not despair, old friend. Even though he was able to break the walls of the southern bastions, his army will be be funnelled into a very small space, where his numbers will mean nothing."

"Wellington unnerves you, too," Gerard persisted. "I can see it in your face."

"Well, of course he does!" Philppon begrudgingly confessed. "He soundly defeated Junot, Massena, Girard, Joseph Bonaparte, he's even thrashed Marshal Soult no less than four times! But if he wants to take Badajoz, he will have to wade through a river of blood and tears."

Gerard and the other French officers had done their best to reassure their men, as well as those citizens who corroborated with them, that Badajoz was impenetrable. After all, two previous attempts to take it had failed. And yet, something was different about this British officer who now faced them. He was calculated, precise, and above all, relentless. Though combined French forces in Portugal had him badly outnumbered, they had never been able to mass their numbers effectively. Wellington's use of terrain and maneuver allowed him to engage only when the odds best suited him. And though he'd most often had to deal with superior French manpower, he'd decisively beaten them time and again. With the French completely driven from Portugal, and the stronghold of Ciudad Rodrigo now in British hands, only Badajoz stood in the way of Wellington's onslaught.

"I daresay, Soult must be anxious to exact his revenge," Gerard conjectured.

Philippon snorted in reply. "If we can hold long enough, he may very well get it." He then met his subordinate's confused stare. "Oh, yes, Marshal Soult has not abandoned us just yet. A messenger was able to sneak through the British lines last night. Soult is about a week's march away with an army of thirty thousand men. Wellington may have us surrounded, but out there he is completely exposed."

"If we know Soult is coming, then so does Wellington," Gerard guessed.

"In which case he will launch his assault long before he is ready," Philippon asserted. "The British army will break on our walls like a red tide."

"I hope you're right," the colonel replied, letting out a deep sigh, which Philippon was quick to notice.

"I am sorry about Marius," he said after a minute. "He was a good soldier. Beastly bad luck, that."

"He was the last of my family's line," Gerard remarked. "He was my brother's only son, and you know Déjà and I have no children. We were so happy to finally serve together. You know he'd been made a captain just a week ago." There was a tear in his eye as he looked back at his superior. "I still remember my brother dressing him in a little soldier's uniform when he was a boy. And now that uniform has brought about his death. He was so young."

"They all are," Philippon replied. "I do not mean to disrespect your loss; as I said, I am sorry for you. Your nephew was twenty-six, which is still a few years older than most of our men. Wars have always been fought by the young; they always will be."

# Chapter III: Agonized Suspense
## 5 April 1812, 4:00 p.m.

Sir Thomas Picton

James had taken the advice of a bugler from the Light Division's Forlorn Hope and taken a plunge in the river, where he gave himself a thorough scrubbing. As the bugler had said, it was best to die clean. Though the water was freezing, he did feel rather refreshed when he donned his uniform once more. As he walked past a nearby grove of trees, he spotted Lieutenant Benedict Harvest for the first time that day. Benedict was sitting on a tree stump, serenely eating an orange. At twenty years of age, he looked more like a schoolboy who should have been studying for his exams, than an officer in the King's army who about to lead his men into hellfire and death.

"Afternoon, Mr. Webster," he said with a tip of his hat.

"And to you, sir," James replied as he sat on a fallen log nearby. The bark of a cannon startled him, though Benedict seemed not to notice.

"You know," Benedict said between bites of his orange, "William Mackie led the Forlorn Hope at Ciudad Rodrigo. Picton has yet to reward him properly, but I think that is because Mackie is a Connaught Ranger."

It was no secret that Sir Thomas Picton despised the Connaught Rangers due to a series of bad behaviours, though some also wondered if it was because it was an Irish regiment. He appreciated their tenacity and valour, but abhorred their conduct off the battlefield. It was not that they were any more or less well behaved than other regiments, but rather when breaches in discipline occurred, they just happened to get caught. Soon after taking command, Picton had a pair of Connaught Rangers flogged in front of the entire division for having stolen a goat. As looting was a capital offense, he'd further chastised the men. They should think themselves lucky to have faced the lash rather than the hangman's noose.

"Whatever Picton's issue with the Rangers," Benedict added, "the important fact is Mackie led the Forlorn and *survived*." Despite his reasoning and attempts at reassuring both himself and his friend, Benedict's words rang hollow.

"But we won't, will we?" James asked rhetorically.

Benedict shook his head. "No, I don't think so. You might, but I think my string of luck has finally run out."

In both love and war, Benedict had always been the lucky one, according to his friends. At Ciudad Rodrigo, he had been scaling the rampart right in the path of the French cannon; yet when the weapon fired, the entire blast of canister shot had gone right over his head. During the same engagement, a Frenchman had had him dead to rights with his bayonet over Benedict's heart. Thinking it would be more amusing to shoot the young officer, he squeezed the trigger on his musket, only to have it fail to fire. This had given Benedict enough time to knock his opponent's weapon aside and drive his sword into the man's throat.

And just the week prior, when the defenders of Badajoz launched a raid to disrupt the siege works, two musket balls passed through the sides of his frock coat, another knocking his hat from his head; and yet the young lieutenant had not so much as been scratched. When the attackers were driven back, he'd drawn his pistol and fired a parting shot at one of their officers. Even though he was right-handed and had fired the weapon from his left, he still scored a precise hit on the back of the man's head, blowing brain matter over his retreating men at a range that should have been impossible with a pistol. This elicited raucous cheers from the men and had even gotten an accolade from the colonel. Benedict never did say whether the shot was deliberate or just a matter of his ever-present luck. Even his name being drawn for leading the Light Division into the Santa Maria breach was no surprise to his friends, who assumed that his fortunes would hold. Some even jokingly told him that he'd likely be a field marshal by the time he was thirty.

In matters of love, Benedict had proven as skilful with the ladies as he was at staying alive in battle. John Cooke told James a story about how Benedict artfully wooed an exceptionally attractive dowager who was nearly twice his age. When later introduced to the lady's daughter, who, ironically, was also older than Benedict, he successfully made his way into her bed as well. James also personally witnessed the young man make off with the niece of a Spanish lord. He was the perfect Casanova; a true gentleman, who only pursued the most beautiful ladies of class and was always successful. And now, after barely a score of years on earth, Benedict Harvest was convinced that his luck was about to run out.

"My mind is made up," he said. "I am certain to be killed."

"Lieutenant Webster!"

The call distracted James from Benedict's mournful prediction. He looked up to see it was Corporal Shanahan. The two officers stood and returned the salute Shanahan rendered.

"Sergeant Davis' compliments," he said. "He asked me to send for you and to deliver this dispatch."

It was a simple folded note that read,

*Assault postponed until the morrow.*

"Well, Benedict," he said, "it looks like your luck has held for at least one more day."

Though Wellington was anxious to take Badajoz, he knew that one extra day would give the artillery time to work another breach in between the first two. Philippon had been busy reinforcing the Trinidad and Santa Maria with all manner of hellish devices, such as buried spikes, caltrops, mines, and any variety of implements that would inflict fearful losses upon any assault force. He also knew that Soult would not be in any better position to relive Badajoz in a single day, so he had ceded to his engineers' requests.

"An agonizing delay," Wellington noted to his aide, Lord Fitzroy Somerset.

"Hardest on those who'd be first into the breach," the young man replied. "Most have made their peace with God and now have to live an extra day, knowing it simply delays the inevitable."

Wellington nodded in reply. As maddening as it was for him, he still intended to at least be alive when the battle was over, whether the assault went good or ill. The recruitment for the Forlorn Hope was deliberately done on the same day as the attack. With that now postponed a day, there was nothing for the poor bastards to do except dwell on their fate.

"Make sure those men have the day off tomorrow as well," Wellington ordered. "And give each an extra half ration of gin before the battle. Drunken scourges they may be, they still seem to have a steadier hand and shoot straighter when they've had a snort."

"Very good, my lord," Somerset replied with a grin.

# Chapter IV: An Uneasy Calm
## 5 April 1812, evening

Contemporary depiction of a Spanish militiaman and Highlander corporal

The sun was setting, but instead of making their way to the breaches, the British army remained in camp. Men sat in small groups around the fires, cooking their dinner and talking quietly amongst themselves. For James Webster and the rest of the Forlorn Hope, it was particularly strange.

"Feels like we should already be dead," a private said as they watched the last rays of the sun set, leaving them in utter blackness.

Though nothing had been said beforehand, the members of the Forlorn had congregated and elected to mess together. As the private had eluded, to their companions in their units it was like they were already dead. Granted, when the assault did come, there would be many casualties amongst the line regiments. Yet for the Forlorn Hope, death was far more of a certainty.

They were all volunteers, each with his reasons for asking to join. In an army that numbered in the tens of thousands, it was easy to find a couple hundred men who simply wished to die. Some were deserters who'd been caught and given the chance at a full pardon, if they should volunteer. Their only other option was a far more certain death by hanging. Here, at least, they had a fighting chance at living. Others had events in their lives take a turn for the worse, and death seemed preferable to carrying on. For them, falling in battle was far better than putting a pistol to their head. At least this way they could die with honour. Still, there were those who simply wished to get at the frogs first. Not all were anxious for death, and a few thought perhaps they could make a name for themselves by surviving such a harrowing experience. A single officer was required to lead each assault, and those who put their names in were often the ones who were far younger and devoid of patronage or ample funds. For them, this offered a chance at rapid career advancement or, at the worst, an honourable death that would bring credit to their family names.

When he first received the letter regarding his wife, James had immediately gone and submitted his name to the list of officers wishing to lead the Forlorn. He acted impulsively, not really conscious of what he was asking for. Now, he wasn't certain he wished to so readily hand his life over to the merciless fates, but it was too late to take it back.

He sat on a fallen tree outside the line of tents. He held an open locket in his hand, and in the faint glow of the firelight, he could see the enclosed picture of his wife. It was a smaller replica of a portrait his father had commissioned when they were engaged. Though he told James in private that he disapproved of him marrying so soon and just before heading off to war, he'd always doted on his daughter-in-law. He and James' mother always treated Amy with much affection, and she was never aware of their misgivings about marrying their son and going with him to Portugal. In truth, they were more worried about what would happen to her, should James fall in battle.

As the enormity of his loss set in, James turned his thoughts towards his daughter, his little Amy. He had never seen her, and yet, now, all he wanted was to hold her, to tell her that he loved her, and he would always be there for her. He would never hold his beloved wife again. And in that moment of realization, his daughter came to mean everything to him. It gave him a reason to live, which in turn overwhelmed him with a sense of hopelessness. He was struck with the stark reality that he would likely never see her. She would grow up devoid of both mother and father.

James ran his thumb over his wife's image in the locket, as the tears he had suppressed all day finally came. They ran freely down his cheeks, and when he was practically blinded by them, he pressed his lips to Amy's picture, closed the locket, clasped it in his fist, and held it up to his forehead as he closed his eyes and cried as quietly as he was able.

The snapping of a twig startled him. He quickly looked over his shoulder, but could not make out the silhouette that was stumbling towards him. All he could make out was the light of the fires that glowed from behind the wall of tents.

"Oh, bugger," the voice of Benedict Harvest said. "I'm sorry, James, I did not mean to disturb you."

"Not at all," James replied, furiously trying to wipe away his tears.

The glow of firelight reflected off the locket, catching his friend's attention.

"I remember you first showing me that," Benedict noted. He stood awkwardly for a moment before continuing. "I am sorry. I was so wrapped up in my self-piteous predictions of my own fate that I neglected to even note your loss. I mourn with you, yet I also envy you."

"What do you mean?" James asked, unsure of the meaning. In his moment of deepest sorrow, he did not see how anyone could possibly envy him.

"What I mean," Benedict said as he took a seat on a nearby stump, "is Amy had your complete devotion and you hers. You had something that I've never experienced, and that is love."

"Benedict, you've been with more women than any of us can count," James retorted, drawing a smile from his friend in the darkness. "You have their admiration; they adore you!"

"Of course they do," Benedict conceded. "But admiration and adoration are not love. As young as I am, it's not unexpected that love is unknown to me. One usually has time to find such things, but not me, not with what we are to do tomorrow. And if I am to die tomorrow, I would trade all the experiences I've had, with all the women I've bedded, just to feel for one brief moment what you and Amy had."

There was a long silence that followed. Under most circumstances this would have been an awkward conversation to have. Benedict would have faced unending ridicule if he were to ever publicly state that he'd trade his experiences of conquering women of class just to know for a moment what it felt like to be loved. But now, with oblivion bearing down on him, he had to let someone know. As they sat in silence, Benedict looked down and shook his head.

"I'm sorry," he finally said. "I came to see how you were managing, and yet I made this about myself once again."

"I don't hold it against you," James said, leaning forward and placing a hand on his friend's shoulder. Knowing Benedict's predicament did not necessarily make him feel better. However, it did make him thankful for the time he and Amy had together. "What say if we do survive tomorrow, you find yourself a nice young lady whose attraction is more than just getting into her bed?"

"I'd like that very much," Benedict replied. "Well, let's see if my luck holds up one more day." He stood and started to walk back to camp. He then abruptly stopped and turned back towards his friend once more. "James, I want you to know that if only one of us does survive, I hope it's you. Your daughter needs her father far more than the duchess' daughter needs me in her bed."

Gerard was scarcely able to sleep at night. He knew the British assault would come sooner rather than later. With Marshal Soult advancing, Wellington was unable to redeploy his army to face him without lifting the siege. In doing so, he would have Soult in front and Philippon behind him.

What particularly vexed Gerard on this night was the loss he'd incurred on the day he sent a raiding party to pilfer the British entrenching tools. The bodies of the dead still lay where they fell; out in a stretch of land that neither French nor British dared to venture. A week had passed, and the corpses had started to bloat, with a pungent smell of death permeating the landscape. In the darkness he could not see the bodies, yet he knew exactly where his nephew had fallen. Though married, Gerard was childless, his late brother's son being the last of their line. He'd scarcely been able to contain his pride when the young man received his commission. Gerard had viewed it as an even greater stroke of fortune that, by chance, they both ended up at Badajoz.

The young officer, anxious to make an impression on his uncle, as well as Baron Philippon, volunteered to lead the raid on the British entrenchments. Successful though they'd been, it had cost him his life. The image was burned into Gerard's mind as he watched a British officer make what should have been an impossible shot with a pistol. Time seemed to stand still, and though the distance was too far for Gerard to actually see, in his mind he could envision the look of pain on his nephew's face in the instant his life ended.

Despite Philippon's reassurances, Gerard was feeling less confident in their ability to hold against the British. And while he held the highest respect for Marshal Soult, Wellington had already beaten him several times! It was strange to Gerard that he felt Soult arriving to relieve Badajoz would actually be a worse scenario than where they were now. To trap Wellington between their two forces would mean facing him in open battle rather than behind thirty-foot walls. Were they fighting Prussians, Austrians, Russians, Spanish, or Portuguese, he would have relished the opportunity. The British army was a different beast altogether. Though barely holding onto their discipline, slow to move, and unable to survive or maintain any semblance of order without their extensive logistics lines, by God they could fight! Only Napoleon's Imperial Guard showed the same kind of iron discipline and cool-headed courage in battle. Gerard hazarded, if Napoleon ever turned his attention to Wellington, a clash between those two would be a battle for the ages.

# Chapter V: Before the fall
## 6 April 1812

Contemporary depiction of a Spanish guerrilla and English soldier

James did not remember falling asleep. It was almost 9:00 in the morning, and yet no one had come to wake him. In his groggy state, he somehow remembered his men were given this day off, as they had been the day before. He would not be required to get accountability until sometime in the late afternoon. And no one would bother him until then. Because, like the private had said the night prior, to their friends they were already dead. It was a strange feeling, especially knowing his body should already be a cold and bloody slab; his soul sent to wherever God saw fit.

It was this last thought that struck him as he opened his personal chest and saw, on top of his uniforms, a small Bible his mother had given him before he left for Portugal. He'd scarcely opened it, not being very religious. He believed in God, as well as the tenets of Heaven and Hell. It was the idea of religion commanding men's lives the way it did that he had little use for. He was thankful his parents were Protestants, and being as he was the youngest of their sons, they had not the energy to force the church upon him when he was young.

The utter arrogance of the Catholic papacy disgusted him, though he kept his loathing of the Pope to himself, especially in front of the Irish soldiers who were overwhelmingly Catholic. Unlike many of his fellow English officers, he actually liked the Irish. In fact, he was rather fond of the people, as well as their country. And rather than holding their Catholicism against them, he pitied them for it. In his mind, it was strange that many Irishmen would wish to free themselves from the rule of King George, and yet they would willingly allow themselves to be slaves to Pius VII, who had been at Napoleon's coronation before being expelled by the French.

The day before, after a few of his friends and fellow officers knew he received word of Amy's death, he had an altercation with a Catholic vicar. James had not sought the man's counsel, yet he took it upon himself to tell the grieving officer that he had to accept his wife's passing as the will of God. Such assertions enraged James, and it had taken the direct intervention of Captain Roberts to stop him from challenging the man to a duel. Duelling was not only forbidden by Wellington and a court-martial offense, but the killing of a priest by an English officer would have sat ill with the Irish Catholics who made up almost a third of the army.

James gave a morbid chuckle at the thought as he thumbed randomly through the Bible.

*'O Lord, God of my salvation, I have cried day and night before thee'...Psalm 88*

"Many of us will cry before the Lord before this deed is done," he said quietly as he placed the Bible back into his chest. He then donned his best frock coat, trousers, and brushed off his bicorn hat. He figured if he was to die this evening, he may as well make a good show of it.

He took a quiet walk through the camp. Many soldiers sat writing notes, which they would then hand to one of their friends, often accepting one in return. Those without wives or children were bequeathing their worldly possessions, what little most of them had, to their mates in the hopes that at least one of them would survive. If, by misfortune, both men should fall, their personal property would often be looted by opportunists, while their military gear would be turned in to the quartermasters. Those who could not read and write were dictating their wishes to friends who could. Yet what was surprising was that, despite much of the army coming from the bottom scrapings of British society, there had been an explosion in literacy during the first part of the 19$^{th}$ Century. It was not uncommon to see the lowly son of a farmer, who'd spent his own days toiling in unskilled labour when he was sober enough to work, that could also read and write.

As James strolled past the rows of tents, he saw companies in formation, being briefed by their officers and non-commissioned officers. Though Wellington had indirectly allowed the men to plunder Ciudad Rodrigo, the outrages committed by the ranks surpassed that of simply looting. The citizenry had been assaulted, women raped, and townsfolk driven into the streets, many of them naked, whilst the British army took them for everything they owned, killing those who resisted. Wellington hoped to avoid such atrocities in Badajoz. Though with such a monumental task that was sure to inflict heavy losses on his men, he feared that his army, in its rage, would subsequently rape and burn the entire city to the ground. It was due to this concern that officers were emphasizing to the men that such actions would not be tolerated. As James continued his walk, he saw his own company formed up in front of their tents. Captain Roberts was reciting the orders passed down to him, while the two company sergeants and their corporals walked the line, stressing the penalties for such gross infractions.

*"There will be no repeating of the despicable behaviour that was seen in Ciudad Rodrigo! Property is to be respected, as are the bodies of the women. Anyone caught looting civilian property, committing assaults upon citizens of Badajoz, or engaging in other acts of destruction will be summarily executed by hanging at the place of their crime! Do your duty, defeat the French, but do not thieve, kill the locals, or submit your heathen desires upon their women, lest you wish to feel the noose around your neck!"*

James knew, although discipline was fierce in the British army, it was a vain threat; one that would prove impossible to enforce, should the entire army lose control of its senses. He had seen a touch of what these men were capable of at Ciudad Rodrigo, and it terrified him. French soldiers attempting to surrender were mercilessly cut down, the citizens cruelly treated, the women violated, and in some cases murdered when they tried to resist. The fact that decent human beings could become more savage than wild beasts showed the depths to which war could shatter one's soul. Even Wellington was rumoured to have said that his own men scared him on occasion.

Though the army drilled them, through rigid discipline, into the most capable fighting force in the world, there was the likelihood that the horrors they would soon face would drive even the most stoic of them completely mad. It was hoped that with two practicable breaches blown in the walls, Philippon would realize he could not possibly hold and would, therefore, surrender honourably. Wellington was magnanimous to a defeated foe and would show clemency to the French.

Observers had noted that far from contemplating surrender, the French were fortifying their defences and laying fearful obstacles in the breaches, to include spikes, as well as rows of sword blades ran through long boards and chained to the rocks. Mines were buried with their long fuses running back to the ramparts. Baron Philippon was gambling on the strength of Badajoz, knowing the breaches were the only real way in. Plus he had to know that Marshal Soult was coming to his aid. Were he to surrender now, it was doubtful that Napoleon would ever forgive him. So, in reality, Wellington could not fault Philippon for standing his ground; he hazarded that were the roles reversed, he would have done the same. This left Wellington with two scenarios, both unnerved him. If he failed to take the city, his entire campaign would be undone with the arrival of Soult, and his own force depleted. Conversely, a victory in Badajoz would come at a high cost and possibly lead to his men unleashing their fury even worse than at Ciudad Rodrigo.

James was very much aware of Wellington's concerns, as they were felt by all officers and non-commissioned officers in the army. However, in that moment, as he gazed at his company, who for the first time he would not be fighting beside, he was not even thinking about what they would do once inside Badajoz. His thoughts were on how many would live to see the following dawn, and would he ever see any of them again? For all he knew, he could be dead long before his company even assaulted the breach. As his focus was on the Forlorn Hope, he did not know which regiments made up each wave of the attack. He guessed that within the first hour it would no longer matter, as all units would most likely be stacked on top of each other in a flurry of destruction as they attempted to break the stronghold. But for that moment, they were still his lads. It made him chuckle that he often referred to the men in the ranks as *lads*, seeing as how many were older than him, with a couple having sons his age. Like every war before this one, the actual fighting was mostly done by the young. James had seen the roles and knew that accounting for the old veterans, as well as new recruits, the average age of rankers within the British army was approximately twenty-three. He surmised that this was probably true of the French as well. James had often looked into the faces of his fallen enemies and saw not men, but young boys staring lifelessly at him.

Some of the men noticed him as he stood watching them with his hands clasped behind his back. A few nodded solemnly and smiled sadly at their officer, who in their minds should have already passed into eternity. James knew many of them would fall and never rise again, so he took just a moment to try and seer the memory of them into his mind. He then touched his hat and continued on his way. Captain Roberts was still giving his speech and had not noticed his subaltern. James preferred it that way. He'd already said his goodbyes to his friend and mentor.

At the edge of the enormous camp, he came across a couple of men he recognized as part of the Forlorn Hope, though like most, he did not know their names. They were debating enthusiastically, and each had a flask that he was using with great emphasis. They immediately ceased in their banter and rose to their feet when they saw their officer approaching.

"Mister Webster," one of the men said.

"Gentlemen," James replied. "You're with the Forlorn?"

"Yes, sir," the private answered. "Private William Lawrence, sir. This here's Private John Reynolds."

"What have you there?" James nodded to their flasks, and Lawrence was quick to explain.

"Gin ration, sir," he answered. "We was given a bit of extra, seeing as how the whole of the army views us as heroes for offering to die a few minutes before the rest of them does. Well, sir, we's debating over whether we should treat ourselves now and risk being sobered up by the time we go into the breach, or do we wait and risk being thoroughly pissed when the attack comes?"

"Just priming the pan on one's musket is the devil when you can't even see it properly," Reynolds added. "Still, I'd rather die sauced and not knowing a frog had got the best of me."

James tried to keep his face stoic, though he found the debate rather amusing.

"A profound decision," he remarked. "Quite possibly the last important one any of us will ever make. Carry on."

"Sir!" both men said as they snapped their heels together.

The day was pleasant, and James debated if he should bathe once more. A fresh scrub and his best uniform would do much to invigorate him. He also needed something to pass the time, as the wait for the day to lapse was maddening. He reached up and felt on his chest where he always kept the locket with his wife's picture beneath his shirt. But then he remembered that it was not there. Should he fall, he wanted it to go to his daughter, and he knew that the corpse of a slain officer would be among the first plundered after a battle, regardless of who the victors were. One survivor from the Forlorn Hope at Ciudad Rodrigo told them of how one of his friends had fallen valiantly as they overwhelmed the French cannon crews. The next morning, his body was found stripped completely naked. James had thought to leave the locket with either Captain Roberts or even with the colonel. Yet, as there was a chance that whoever he left it with would also fall, he saw little point in leaving it with anyone. Instead, he'd left it in his chest with a note attached, imploring whoever took hold of his possessions to show enough decency to send the locket home to his daughter and his Bible to his mother. They were free to take the remainder of his worldly possessions, with his compliments.

Near a small copse of trees, he spotted one of his non-commissioned officers, cleaning his musket and sorting through his ammunition cartridges.

"Corporal Shanahan, is it?" James asked, startling the man and causing him to jump to his feet.

"Lieutenant, sir!" he said quickly. "Beg your pardon, did not see you there."

"No harm done," James replied, waving for him to return to his task.

"Sir, if I may say," Shanahan stated as he started to place cartridges into his ammunition pouch, "I'm awfully glad you didn't try and duel with the vicar. Bad bit of luck that would have brought from the Almighty, what with us going into the breach and all."

46

"Well, I cannot expect my actions to be viewed favourably by the Irish Catholics," James conceded.

"Catholic?" Shanahan said with a touch of surprise. "Oh no, sir, I'm not a Catholic. I have but one master of this world, and he's not the Pope. No, sir, King George is all the ruling I can take. I do still put my trust in the Lord, blessed be his name." He then crossed himself and looked up at the sky briefly before continuing. "The vicar is a good man, and he means well, even if his words may not have been appropriate, sir."

"Why are you here, corporal?" James asked with a change of subject.

"Me, sir?" Shanahan replied with a shrug. "I suppose it's because someone has to go in first, and I figured I could not very well ask one of me lads to do so, so I went in their place. Damn silly thing, really."

"So, not anxious to die then, are you?"

"Not at all, sir," Shanahan replied with a chuckle. "No, me wife would frown upon that considerably."

"You're married then?" James asked, not sure why he should be surprised. He surmised that the corporal was a few years older than him, so it would not be unusual.

"Oh yes, sir," he answered. "Got me three little ones too; a son and twin daughters. They's at home in Ireland. We live near a little village called Sixmilebridge; a funny name, that. I was not going to have my children raised in war, and so while many other soldiers' wives were trying to get onto the army roles so they could accompany their husbands into Portugal, me wife and I elected that she would remain in Ireland with our children. I do miss her every day, though. Beg your pardon, sir, I should not complain."

James nodded sadly. After his altercation with the vicar, any hope of keeping his loss a secret to the men in the ranks was gone. They knew why he was there, and his heart suddenly stabbed with the pain at missing his beloved Amy. He had shed his tears the night before, but the lingering ache would remain for some time. Even if he did live through the assault, it would still be there to temper any feelings of relief he would have about surviving.

It was not just the British who were filled with trepidation regarding the fate of them and their wives. For Gerard, that his wife, Déjà, had elected to visit him could not have happened at a worse time. Her stay was meant to only last a week or so, as she wished to see her husband and nephew. Now she was trapped by the British army, and should Badajoz fall, her fate would be far more terrifying than that of her husband. Gerard felt the same fears that all soldiers did before battle; however, he accepted his fate, whether the city held or not. It was a risk all accepted once they donned the uniform. His greatest fear now was that he would be killed and unable to protect his wife should the British carry the bastions.

The streets were quiet, with the exception of the occasional bursting of stone and metal as enemy cannon continued to hammer the ramparts. Gerard held his wife's hand as they walked to the nunnery. He'd already made arrangements with the mother superior. His wife would stay at the nunnery in their care, should the British attack come that day. It was heart-wrenching for Déjà, and tears streaked her face as her husband ran his fingers gently through her hair.

"Every day we come here," she said with a broken voice. "And every day I fear I will never see you again."

"This is the safest place for you," Gerard assured her. "I do not think even the English will dare defile a holy place like this. Whatever happens to me, the sisters here have promised to protect you."

Déjà swallowed hard and nodded in understanding. She kissed her husband passionately and held him close for the few moments they had. She then abruptly turned and followed a nun, who gently guided her through the door of the convent.

Gerard sighed and fought back his own emotions. His family had already suffered much tragedy over the past year. Though his elderly parents still lived, they'd lost a son to typhus the previous winter. With the British entrenched around Badajoz, there was no way of letting them know their only grandson was also dead. Gerard wondered if they were damned to lose their remaining son, as well as their daughter-in-law, before this hateful affair was over.

"How is she?" Philippon asked when Gerard reported for duty at the castle that morning.

"A bit shook up," the colonel admitted. "War is no place to bring one's wife."

"That she would come, even knowing what happened at Ciudad Rodrigo, speaks well for her courage," Philippon reasoned.

"She is a brave one, there's no doubt about that," Gerard agreed. "She risked coming all the way through Spain just to spend a few days with me and our nephew. I had not seen her since the English landed their expeditionary forces nearly four years ago, and she reasoned it might be our last opportunity. In that, she may have been right."

Gerard received his orders of the day and decided to take a walk along the ramparts of the Trinidad bastion, as they were his responsibility. The breach blown by the British siege guns was impressive and a tribute to their utter relentlessness. The defenders had taken much of the rubble and built a waist-high wall a few yards back from the breach. Here is where Gerard designated the majority of his infantry. He had men along what remained of the walls, as well as crews for each of the cannon that were all sighted in on the far side of the trench, from where they knew the British would have to approach.

"Colonel, sir," a sentry greeted him.

Gerard looked over the short wall and down the slope that was now infested with spikes and mines. He shook his head and wondered if anyone could be foolish enough to try and assault through that.

"They won't get through here," the soldier asserted, matching Gerard's own thoughts.

And yet, for all the hellish manner of traps plus the enfilade fields of fire offered to his cannon and infantry, something still unsettled the colonel. Any other army would have given up on taking something as impenetrable as Badajoz, yet the English persisted. Gerard knew Wellington had never been beaten in a major battle and would not be continuing the siege if he did not think his soldiers could break the stronghold. Philippon knew this as well; hence, they were committing every resource they had to holding the bastions. If even one part of the defences cracked, there would be no stopping the surge of redcoats.

# Chapter VI: Into the Breach
## La Trinidad bastion, Badajoz
### 6 April 1812

"God be with you."

"God be with the Forlorn Hope."

Such phrases were quietly echoed from the assault groups as James and his band of valiant volunteers followed their guide to the trenches that led them towards Badajoz and their destiny. The sun had fallen a couple hours prior, and all was black. All they could hear was the shuffling of their feet over the damp earth, as well as their own nervous breathing.

At length they climbed out of the last trench and made their way quietly across the open plain. Regiments that would follow them into the breach were assembled; most of the men were kneeling next to their assault ladders and grass bags. By chance, they passed his own company from the 3rd Battalion of the 1st Foot Guards. James recognized the hushed voice of one of the men.

"Return to us a captain, sir."

He smiled briefly at the notion, though quickly dismissed the thought from his mind. He then wondered how many lads from his company would fall this night. They would be in the first assault, right behind the Forlorn Hope. In real terms, the only difference was they might live a few minutes longer before being cut down over the bodies of Lieutenant Webster and the volunteers of the damned.

His guide halted abruptly, and James almost bumped into him. He then glanced to his right and saw that the man had been stopped by his captain, Daniel Roberts. Though they had already said goodbye and wished each other well, seeing his friend pass by him in the quiet night that preceded the coming storm proved too much for the captain. The two men clasped hands, and it was then James noticed Daniel's face was streaked with tears. No words needed to be spoken. James placed a reassuring hand on his friend's shoulder and then signalled for the guide to continue.

Knowing the ditch surrounding Badajoz was deep, with a steep precipice, men not bearing ladders carried large bags of grass that they would use to break their falls when they jumped in. Sergeant Davis crept along next to Lieutenant Webster, carrying such a sack, his rifle slung over his shoulder. Behind them were Corporal Shanahan and the ever-present Privates Lawrence and Reynolds. In the black of night it was hard for James to make out where anything was. His guide from the 95th Rifles seemed sure of himself, and so he placed all of his trust in the man. Those selected to act as guides had thoroughly reconnoitred their avenues of approach over the past few days, rehearsing their approaches both during the day, as well as at night. For James and his men, the faint light that came from Badajoz was the only thing that told him if they were moving in the right direction.

Eventually, they reached a designated halting point that was about one hundred yards from the ditch. The guide stopped and dropped to a knee. James kept low as he knelt down beside the man. The rest of the Forlorn Hope halted and assessed the imposing fortress they now had the daunting task of leading the assault upon.

"La Trinidad bastion," the rifleman whispered. "You may not be able to see it yet, but if you go straight on and keep the lights of the castle in your sights and just off to your right, you'll find your breach."

"Much obliged to you, sir," James said as he shook the man's hand.

"And to you, sir," the rifleman replied before rising up and heading back to his regiment. The 95th Rifles would be assaulting the Santa Maria bastion off to their left where, at that moment, Lieutenant Benedict Harvest and his men were forming up.

James took a minute and steeled himself to his task. It was hard to see much in the utter blackness. The occasional torch from French sentries silhouetted the ramparts, which were staggering in their size. He wondered how long they would last, a minute…two, perhaps? Would they even get into the breach before they were all cut to pieces? No trumpets or fanfare accompanied the Forlorn Hope, only silent courage. Even though more than twenty-thousand men would eventually converge on the assault, for a brief instant forever etched in time, Lieutenant James Webster and his men were utterly alone. In that moment of silence he said a quick prayer, in case God happened to be listening. He prayed not for survival, but for a mercifully quick death. And with the last pleadings of his very soul he asked that fate be kinder to his daughter than it had been to her parents.

"We ready to do this, sir?" Sergeant Davis asked quietly.

51

James gave a nod and drew his sword.

"Let's get it over with."

To the north of where the 4<sup>th</sup> and Light Divisions made ready to storm the breach, Major General Thomas Picton was preparing to personally lead the 3<sup>rd</sup> Division in the assault on the castle. At first glance, theirs was perhaps the most daunting task of all. The castle was by far the most fortified point of Badajoz, with walls thirty to forty feet high in places. There were no breaches blown in the walls here. Picton and his men would simply have to scale the siege ladders in the hope that some of them would reach the top before being shot, and without their ladders being tipped over. So perilous was their mission, it wasn't even supposed to succeed. Rather, it was simply a diversion, as was Sir James Leith and the 5<sup>th</sup> Division's assault on the San Vincente bastion to the west. Wellington's focus was still on the breaches that his siege guns had spent weeks working over until they were practicable.

The abject futility of their mission was not lost on the men of the 3<sup>rd</sup> Division, though their commanding general was not to be dissuaded. He had boasted to Wellington that his men would be first into Badajoz, and he intended to make good on his promise. In the blackness, he could not see his way and could scarcely make out his guide. He swore he would beat the man senseless if he led them to the wrong spot.

Sir Thomas Picton was a crass old general. He berated his soldiers constantly; referring to them by all sorts of names that made Wellington's *'scum of the earth'* moniker sound almost like a term of endearment. Picton's language was often coarse, like those of the rankers, laced with all manner of colourful profanity. While his vile speech and questionable conduct was unbecoming of a gentleman in Wellington's eyes, there was no denying Picton's talent or personal courage. At the Battle of Fuentes de Onoro the year previously, and later at Ciudad Rodrigo, Picton's valour and tactical savvy contributed decisively to the British victories, enhancing his own reputation, as well as that of *The Fighting 3<sup>rd</sup>*.

So while his men had absolutely no love for him, they did respect him. The fact that he was personally leading the assault, and thereby sharing in the same hazards as his men, led many to forgive the general for his crassness. Picton was no fool, though. Like Wellington, he often went into battle dressed in plain civilian garb, knowing his general officer's uniform was so conspicuous he would have every French gun trained on him. He guessed, in such circumstance, he wouldn't survive thirty seconds once the shooting began.

# Chapter VII: The Cauldron of Hell
## Trinidad bastion, Badajoz, 10 p.m.

It was time. Once James told Sergeant Davis, '*Let's get it over with*', his mind became instinctive and all emotion left him. The time for prayers and thoughts of family and friends was done. It was time to do his duty and accept the extreme probability of not living to see the dawn. His curved sword was draped over his shoulder, and he hunkered low while keeping an eye out for the ditch. The last thing he wanted was to fall into the sheer drop and break his neck before the first shot was even fired. His footfalls, though softened by the damp earth, echoed loudly in his ears. He felt certain the French would hear them before they got close to the ditch. He could just make out Sergeant Davis' breathing as he hefted the large sack of grass. James quietly hoped the man would not break into another coughing fit before they could launch the assault. The men bearing ladders stumbled along, trying their best to keep in step, lest they fall over each other with a loud crash.

The closer they got to the ditch, the more James' heart raced. He swore it beat so loudly that even the French could hear it. Yet aside from the muffled steps of his men, the only sound in the deathly-still night was the occasional croaking of frogs. Horror coursed through his very soul as the shadow of the ditch came into sight. The silence threatened to swallow him, and he took a series of deep breaths, trying to keep from hyperventilating. This was not his first action, yet the silent darkness unnerved him far more than the roar of muskets and clash of men had at Talavera.

The longer they could go without alerting the French sentries, the further into the breach they would get. Once they reached the ditch, he knew surprise would likely be lost. Though Wellington had ordered all soldiers to leave their packs and most of their equipment behind, their weapons alone would clatter against ladders, as well as the embankment as they initiated the assault. It would then become a mad rush down the ladders or onto the grass sacks, and a race up the far embankment and into the breach.

An explosion off to the left caused his eyes to grow wide, and his breath left him. He realized it was impossible to coordinate his and Lieutenant Harvest's attacks to the exact moment and supposed he

54

should have been thankful they made it to the ditch before the other Forlorn Hope was engaged. The roar and flash of cannon and musket fire on the left shattered the deafening silence.

*"Les voila! Les voila!"* The words of the French sentries echoed along the ramparts.

"Shit," James swore under his breath. Any reputing thoughts towards ungentlemanly language or behaviour became meaningless as the first fire bombs were thrown from behind the French ramparts. With a soft burst of ignition, the burning hulks tumbled down the slope and lit up the area in front of the ditch, highlighting the hundred men who would now live and die by their name, the Forlorn Hope.

*"Let's go!"* James shouted as his men rushed forward.

*"Les voila!"* The shout of the French sentry was followed with a volley of musket fire. A bell started ringing frantically from inside Badajoz, and it would not be long before the rampart was filled with French soldiers. James could see the advancing sparks of lit fuses that were soon followed with the detonation of mines within the breach. He was grateful the defenders had detonated these too soon, but terrified at the notion that there were many more buried right in the path he and his men now had to advance through. The first wave would be starting its advance, and he knew they would be upon them in a matter of a few minutes. His men had to get into the breach quickly! The more detonated mines, and the more cannon and musket fire they took, hopefully the less that would fall upon the first wave.

A scream let him know his command had suffered its first casualty. A soldier on one of the ladders fell to his knees, clutching at his ruptured stomach in utter agony. Sergeant Davis clutched his grass sack to his chest and leapt into the ditch. A loud splash alerted James just as the first cannons within the breach unleashed their fiery torment. A shell burst nearby, knocking down three of the four men who were bearing a ladder. Two were killed instantly, the third lay crying in anguish, his left leg blown off, and his guts spilled upon the earth.

*"The fucking ditch is flooded!"* Sergeant Davis shouted from below. *"God save us!"*

"God has abandoned us," Corporal Shanahan growled as he helped the surviving ladder bearer, Private William Lawrence, hoist

55

his burden and drop it over the side of the ditch. Poor Private Reynolds was one of those slain by the burst of shell.

"Sleep well, you lucky bastard," William said under his breath as he looked back at the shattered and bloody body that had once been his friend.

James was first onto the ladder. He did not bother using the rungs, but simply slid down the sides. He landed in the water with a loud splash and sank clear to the bottom. The water was far deeper than he'd anticipated. He was submerged well over his head, and he started to panic. As he only carried his sword and a pistol with a handful of rounds, he was not nearly as encumbered as many of his men were. How many would sink to the bottom and not rise again, weighted down by muskets and ammunition pouches, he could only guess. And of those who did make it out of the ditch, how many weapons would fail to fire because they were soaked?

As he struggled to make his way to the surface, a pair of boots struck him hard, causing him to sink once more. Fortunately, he did not lose consciousness. His men were jumping into the ditch or sliding down ladders as quickly as they could, often smashing into their companions below. This only added to the chaos as men scrambled over each other in an attempt to keep from drowning. Seeing the plight below, the last dozen or so men of the Forlorn Hope threw their weapons and cartridge belts to the far side of the ditch. Whether they made it to the other side or not, at least someone would have dry weapons with which to shoot back at the enemy.

As James clawed his way out of the ditch, his once-pristine uniform now sodden and filthy, he glanced around and took assessment of the situation. It was already dire. Only he, Sergeant Davis, and maybe five of the lads had made it out of the ditch and onto the embankment near him. Some were trying in vain to fire their water-soaked weapons and cursing feverishly each time one failed to go off.

The lieutenant looked back over his shoulder as a mine detonated near his head, knocking off his bicorn hat and tearing it to pieces. Luckily, it had been buried too deep, and he was splattered with mostly dirt and debris. The situation behind them was quickly turning desperate. From the looks of it, nearly half his men never even made it into the ditch. They lay scattered on the far side, the continuous barrage of burning stick bundles and hay bales illuminating the mangled corpses of the dead and the devastated bodies of the wounded. The few men James had with him could do nothing to silence the cannon that raked the embankment, and he knew the men in the first wave would soon be subjected to its horrible onslaught. Still, more members of the Forlorn continued to claw their way out of the trench, a few picking up the dry weapons that had been tossed over. Their sporadic shots were met with coordinated volleys of murderous fire from the ramparts, as French companies quickly manned their positions.

Behind the rampart, Gerard calmly walked the line. As the alarm bell continued to ring feverishly, his men started to pour onto the rampart. An entire company formed a line, fired a single volley, and then fell behind the protective stoneworks to reload. Cannon continued to thunder and their entire front was socked in with smoke. Return fire from the British attackers was sparse and uncoordinated. He knew that would soon change once the initial wave attacked. For now, all they had to deal with was the handful of advance troops who were always first into the breach. What the British called the Forlorn Hope, the French referred to as *Les Enfants Perdus*, 'the lost children'. The meaning was still the same, and those few who survived would be little more than broken shells of what they'd once been. It was a terrible thing, but the colonel knew that were the roles reversed, the British would show them no mercy.

Gerard felt a sense of calming confidence wash over him. With all manner of hellish traps set in the breach, combined with the massed firepower of his men, the British had no chance of making it into the Trinidad bastion. Those attacking the Santa Maria would fair little better. The thought of the attacks on the San Vincente or the castle having any chance of succeeding was presposterous at best. Attempting to scale the high walls with ladders was a foolhardy endeavor; so much so that Philippon had designated only the minimal amount of defenders necessary to each rampart. The main British effort would come through the two southern breaches, which were virtually impenetrable. Gerard knew then that Badajoz would hold, and the only thing to greet Wellington in the morning would be piles of dead and wounded from his shattered army.

In a secluded room of the nunnery, his wife was not so certain of their safety. It was dark and windowless, with the only light coming from an oil lamp on the small table by the door. As the thunder of cannon reverberated through the walls, Déjà sat on the edge of the bed, rocking back and forth slowly, her eyes shut. A nun sat on the bed next to her and put a reassuring arm around her shoulder.

"They'll not get into the city," the sister said soothingly. "God will protect your husband and those who defend the city."

Déjà looked curiously over at the nun.

"You are all Spanish," she noted. "I would think you'd want the English to succeed."

"We do not concern ourselves with the wars of men here," the sister replied. "Our purpose is to serve God, not man. If the English take the city, there will be much suffering. They are like wild animals when unleashed."

Both had heard about the atrocities committed by the British soldiers at Ciudad Rodrigo, and the Spanish citizens feared what would happen should they take Badajoz. Gerard had reassured her that she would be safe in the nunnery, whatever should happen to him. With nothing but the crash of cannon shaking the building, Déjà could not know if the battle was going good or ill.

She then glanced up at the brass crucifix that hung above the small table. She found it curious that the French and British prayed to the same God. Whose prayers would He answer, or had He simply abandoned this place?

As cannon and musket rang in his ears and deadened his other senses, in a more shallow part of the trench, James could see Corporal Sharp leading a handful of men up the steep climb of sharp rocks to the left of the breach. They rose as one and fired a concentrated volley into the defenders on the rampart. It was the first coordinated blow they'd been able to throw against their enemy, and it was met with a devastating mass of musketry.

"Sir, we have to continue the advance!" Sergeant Davis shouted to him over the din of cannon fire and the detonation of mines.

James nodded and waved to the men with his sword for them to follow him. One threw down his water-logged musket and grabbed one that had been pitched over the ditch. He quickly rose up and fired into the French defences, giving a brief smile of satisfaction at having done something to try and hurt the enemy. Before he could load another round, the return fire of a dozen French weapons tore him to pieces. His eyes glassed over and a stream of blood ran from the corner of his mouth as he fell forward into a twitching heap that had once been a man.

Screams came from men who'd been neither shot nor blasted with mines. The ground was strewn with long spikes, and a number of poor fellows had their hands, feet, and various limbs punctured by the painful devices. James saw one man, clutching his bleeding hand. Another spike had run through the meat of his thigh as well. He looked up at his officer piteously. James grabbed him by the shoulder.

"Come on," he said, "at least death will make the pain stop."

"Yes, sir," the man said through tears and gritted teeth. He wrenched his crippled leg from the spike, and with his good hand, he picked up his musket, bayonet fixed, and limped forward towards the breach. Within seconds, a musket ball smashed through his skull and exploded out of the back, splattering James with the man's skull fragments and brain matter. Knowing there was little to do but keep moving; he turned back towards the breach. He prayed that Benedict Harvest was having a better go at it than he.

The ditch in front of the Santa Maria bastion was not flooded, but for Lieutenant Benedict Harvest, his luck had indeed run out. He and his men had gotten further before being discovered, but as they made their way up the gravelly slope towards the breach, the explosion of a dozen mines shredded him, and those nearest, to ribbons. It was the first explosion James Webster had heard that tore Benedict's soul from his now mangled body.

An officer from the 95<sup>th</sup> Rifles had been his escort to the breach. He had watched intently as the young lieutenant led his men into the trench. For a brief moment, as they scaled the far slope in silence, he thought perhaps they would be able to get into the breach before the first wave assaulted. Like the name implied, it was a forlorn hope, shattered in the blast of mines, followed by the eruption of cannon and musketry. The officer shook his head as the remnants fought valiantly, albeit hopelessly, to get into the breach. He then turned back and jogged the way he'd come, returning to his regiment. As he listened to the sounds of gunfire, accompanied by screams and battle cries, he wondered if any of the Forlorn Hope would still be alive when he returned a few minutes later.

# Chapter VIII: Pathetic Tragedy
## 10:30 p.m.

General Picton became incensed when he heard the sounds of battle coming from the south of his position. Whatever Wellington may have thought about his and Leith's attacks being secondary diversions, he was resolute in his determination that the 3$^{rd}$ Division would take Badajoz. Granted, the 4$^{th}$ and Light Divisions would be bearing the brunt of French resistance; however, they had breaches in the walls to assault through. For Picton, as well as for Leith and his 5$^{th}$ Division, there was no other way into Badajoz than straight up the walls.

"Damn your fucking eyes, man!" Picton growled at the guide with his usual candour and complete disregard for verbal etiquette. "If we are not first into the city because your incompetence got us lost, so help me, I'll flog your arse straight to the gates of hell myself!"

His diatribe was cut short as the guide turned and placed a hand on his shoulder. He signalled for the general to be quiet and then dropped to a knee. Picton did the same as the guide pointed to their front. Barely visible in the utter blackness was the imposing castle.

"Here we are, sir," the guide whispered, "exactly where you directed me to take you."

"Right you are, then," Picton replied as he gave a quick assessment of the wall to his direct front. "That's going to be a bastard to get up."

"That it is, sir," an officer muttered to his right.

Picton glanced over and saw it was Lieutenant William Mackie who'd made the remark. The general raised an eyebrow.

"Lieutenant Mackie," he said.

"Yes, sir?" the young officer replied, keeping his eyes front on the castle.

"You believe I did you wrong by not rewarding you properly for leading the Forlorn Hope at Ciudad Rodrigo."

It was a statement rather than a question.

"If you want my candid response," Mackie replied, "yes, sir, you did me wrong. And if I may continue to be blunt, you have held your grudge against the Connaught Rangers long enough."

"Then it is time for you to prove my assessment wrong," Picton retorted, though his tone was not as biting as usual. "If your bastards prove their mettle against these walls, I will recant my rebuke against the Rangers. And if you, sir, beat me up that climb into death, you will be a captain upon reaching the top."

"Yes, sir," William replied, gritting his teeth in determination.

Picton grinned. He would need such resolve from all of his men if they were to have any chance of taking the castle. He never gave a second thought as to their actual chances; it did not matter. He'd told Wellington they would be the first into the city, and by God, if he could not keep his promise, then his bloodied corpse would suffice in retribution. He then turned and nodded to his bugler. The young man swallowed hard, raised the bugle to his lips, and sounded the attack. A rising shout erupted from the regiments of Picton's division as they swarmed towards the wall.

The first wave fell upon the Trinidad breach with no better results than Lieutenant Webster and the Forlorn Hope. Grapeshot from French cannons tore into their ranks before they even got into the ditch. Others drowned in the deep waters as they struggled against the weight of their equipment, the relentless barrage of enemy fire, and the trampling of their own comrades falling into the trench behind them. James was glad to no longer be so alone in the enemy's cauldron of fire, but at the same time he was remorseful that so many were falling. The Forlorn Hope had completely failed in its mission of gaining a foothold into the breach. All they could do was hide behind what little cover there was, and return sporadic fire at the defences. With his men scattered, and having no notion as to how many could still stand and fight, attempting to coordinate an actual assault was now impossible.

The path into the breach was impenetrable. Chained to the rocks were long wooden planks with sword blades protruding from then. Known to the French as the *chevaux de frise*, they completely blocked the way into the breach. Behind them was a waist-high rampart where defenders knelt behind and fired into the exposed attackers. James watched as Private Lawrence tried in vain to dislodge one of the obstacles. A burst of musket fire tore into him, striking both his legs, as well as his side. At first James thought the young man was fatally stricken, until he held up his dented canteen and simply shook his head. He then tried to regain his footing, oblivious to the wounds in his legs. He could not stand properly and fell onto his back, sliding uncontrollably down the slope. Soldiers were struggling up past him in what James guessed was the second wave. Soldiers of the first, along with what was left of the Forlorn Hope, were engaged in a shooting match with the French defenders. However, as their enemy had a rampart to protect them, with cannon on either side, the hapless British attackers were completely exposed and channelled into the narrow lane that led to the breach. The pungent smoke from burned black powder was thick in the air, and one could not even see the enemy soldiers, only the occasional flash from their weapons. Indeed, the *chevaux de frise* were obscured and a number of hapless souls fell upon them, their bodies eviscerated by the protruding blades. James was secretly thankful for having been practically deafened by the roar of cannon, as he could not hear the screams of the wounded and dying.

Sergeant Davis lay next to him, behind a rock, firing back at the French as best he was able. His Baker rifle took longer to reload, but was far more accurate than the musket. To his left he could see the torn body of Corporal Sharp, sprawled facedown in a pool of blood and gore, along with most of the men he'd led up the steep face. He could not see Corporal Shanahan in the growing clouds of smoke, but he could barely make out the sounds of Irish brogue spewing profanities at the French. Though nearly a third of the British army was made up of Irishmen, James recognized the voice, as it had been swearing nonstop at the French since the attack began. The only times it ceased were in the brief moments it took for the corporal to stand and fire his weapon. As he'd not had time to get to know the men, he had no idea who, if any, were mixed in amongst the soldiers of the various regiments that now crowded into the killing field. For all he knew, he, Davis, Shanahan, and the now-wounded Lawrence were the only ones left. He spotted a couple of green-jacketed riflemen returning fire from amongst the rocks, though he could not tell if they were from the Forlorn or if the 60th Regiment had launched its main assault.

As the first and second assaults foundered, bugles announced the advancing of the third wave. The large rock that provided cover for James and Sergeant Davis was their only salvation. French defenders were focusing more of their fire on it, preventing them from moving. They could no longer move forward or retreat. A handful of soldiers from the first two waves were in similar predicaments; their comrades were either dead, wounded, or having fallen back. In the haze, James recognized off to his right the uniforms of his own regiment. He noted one private from his company, who had just lain down behind a rock to reload his musket. He fumbled with the paper cartridge, which he bit into and with trembling hands, primed the pan and poured the rest of the powder down the barrel and spit in the ball. The soldier then glanced over and recognized his officer.

"Lieutenant Webster, that you?" the man shouted as he withdrew his ramrod and feverishly hammered the ball down the barrel.

"It is," James replied.

"Well fancy that," the private replied as he rolled onto his stomach and fired between the sword blades of the *chevaux de frise* in front of him. He rolled back behind the rock and proceeded to reload. "Looks like I lost a shilling to one of me mates, provided he's still alive. He bet there'd be some of the Forlorn Hope still alive once we hit the breach, and I told him not a chance."

"Your confidence is inspiring!" James retorted over the din of continuous fire as he aimed his pistol towards the rampart and was amazed it went off. He reloaded as fast as his trembling hands would let him, but realizing how useless his weapon was, he stuffed it into his belt and grabbed a musket from a fallen soldier, along with the man's ammunition pouch. As he crawled back behind the rock, grapeshot from a cannon scored his legs. A French musket ball slammed into his thigh, tearing a nasty gash that bled profusely. Yet, so numb was his body from the continuous concussion, James did not even realize he'd been hit.

"Well, sir," the soldier remarked, "forgive my coarse speech, but we're all pretty well fucked anyway. Can't go forward, can't go back. Nothing to do except die in place...which I figured you and the Forlorn had already done. We won't see the dawn, sir, but at least we can make a good show of it before the Lord takes us."

"That we can," James muttered. He then quickly placed his weapon on top the rock and fired off a round. He was shocked when through a break in the smoke he saw a Frenchman's head snap back as the musket ball smashed into his skull. The lieutenant grinned and lay back down behind the rock. "At least I've evened the score for my own death," he said as he bit into a cartridge and primed the pan of the musket. He then poured the rest down the barrel and then spit in the ball.

"You mean you got one?" Sergeant Davis asked with a macabre laugh.

"I did," James replied excitedly as he rammed the bullet home.

"I'd like to avenge my own death before I fall, even if I am fatally ill as it is," the sergeant replied, firing his weapon once more. "Thing is, with all this bloody smoke, I can't see shit. Are we the only ones of the Forlorn left?"

"I don't know," James said with a shake of his head. "Shanahan is still alive...at least I think that's him who's been spewing obscenities for the past half hour."

*"You limp-cocked frog bastards! I'll shag the shit out of every last one of you with a bleeding rusty bayonet!"*

"That'd be him," Davis chuckled with a nod.

Gerard quickly ducked down when he saw the soldier's head snap back, his forehead smashed in by a musket shot. The colonel could not avert his gaze as the man lay twitching on the rampart, blood gushing from the wound, his tongue protruding sickly between his teeth. He knew that he would lose men this night, regardless of the battle's outcome. Still his men fought on, firing as rapidly as they were able to over the rampart. Whatever casualties they suffered, they knew the attackers were taking it far worse. The battle could not be seen due to the thick clouds of smoke and the ever-present darkness of night, but it could be heard and above all, felt. Burning bales of hay and large bundles of flaming stakes were hurled over the ramparts, though their light did little to illuminate the British assaulters through the smoke. Instead, it added an eerie glow to the macabre spectacle. It did not matter. Gerard had instructed his men to shoot in the general direction of the attack, knowing the British would be coming on in massive waves that only made them easier to hit.

Men were laughing gleefully as they continued to fire over the rampart. It was all-too-easy for them.

*"Come on and try again!"* one shouted in broken English, eliciting guffaws from his fellows.

*"Let us welcome you to Badajoz!"* another called out, taunting their trapped enemy.

Gerard gave a satisfied nod and walked to the left end of the rampart, where the cannon were continuing to fire grapeshot at the attackers. Though he was in overall command of the defence of the Trinidad bastion, there was little for him to actually do. His men were doing a fine task of thwarting Wellington's hopes of taking the city. For weeks the defenders had been tormented by the British siege guns, with many being killed or maimed. His men had been driven mad with desire for retribution, and now they were finally able to have their revenge. The attack would fail and once Marshal Soult arrived, they would destroy what was left of the broken British army. In one fell swoop, Wellington would be finished and the British driven from the continent.

Somehow, Private William Lawrence had managed to crawl out of the flooded trench. He'd just made it to the top of the ladder and pulled himself over when he was nearly trampled by oncoming soldiers of the fourth wave. Grapeshot tore into two men nearest him, and as they fell to the earth, crying in pain, he was suddenly glad that all he could do at the moment was crawl. Officers shouted orders as men hurried into the ditch. It was inconceivable that after three assaults, they were no closer to gaining the breach than when the Forlorn Hope had gone in! Far more than inconceivable, it was a pathetic tragedy. He had no idea how the attack on the Santa Maria bastion was progressing, but given the Trinidad assault's complete lack of progress, he hazarded that the Light Division was faring no better.

He crawled over to the musket of a slain soldier. The weapon was smashed and useless, but then William did not need it to fire.

For him, the battle was over, provided he could make it out of range of the French cannon. He struggled to his feet and, using the broken musket as a makeshift crutch, he limped away from the hell storm of battle. A bugle sounded, announcing yet another assault.

"Don't bother, lads," William muttered quietly. "There's nothing to do in Badajoz except die."

Despite the wounds to his legs, he found that using the musket to prop himself up, he could make decent progress, and before long the sounds of the guns and unholy cries of the wounded and dying began to subside. His ears were ringing from the barrage of deafening noise they'd been subjected to and, oddly enough, his side hurt worse than his legs. It kept him doubled over, and he struggled to breathe. After a few minutes of hobbling, the sound of a horse whinnying alerted him. He looked up and saw none other than Wellington himself astride his mount.

"What is your name and regiment, soldier?" the commanding general asked as he rode up to him. Wellington then noted the holes in the thighs of William's trousers, which were soaked in coagulating blood.

"Private William Lawrence," he replied, "40th Regiment, sir. I was with the Forlorn Hope."

"How bad are your injuries, man?" Wellington asked. His tone had softened slightly at hearing William had been a Forlorn Hoper.

"I don't think the doctors will be needing the amputation saws," he answered with a forced smile through gritted teeth. "I do think I'm bleeding pretty good, though." His face grew pale.

Wellington signalled to one of his staff officers. "Help him," he ordered.

"Much obliged, sir," William said as the man guided him to a nearby tree and helped him sit against it.

The officer then started to check his wounds. "Looks like the bullet passed through here. Your other wound will leave a nasty scar, but is mostly superficial."

"And yet my side hurts worse than either," William added, showing his smashed canteen.

The officer gave a sad smile and took a handkerchief to bind the leg wounds.

"One last thing, soldier," Wellington said over his shoulder. "Have any of our men made it into the city?"

"No, sir," William replied with a sad shake of his head. "And if I may be so bold, your grace, I don't think any of us will."

Wellington grimaced and turned his gaze front. The reports coming back had all been the same; although he'd hoped that since a soldier in the Forlorn Hope would be in the best position to see if the breaches could be taken, maybe the official accounts of the attack were prematurely grim. The reports from Picton and Leith were no better, though that was to be expected. After all, their attacks were supplemental, nothing more. If the breaches could not be taken, then the attack on Badajoz would ultimately fail. Hundreds had already fallen, and yet they were no closer to gaining the town than they were when the attack began. With the casualties they'd already suffered, if the assault failed, not only would the morale of his army be shattered, but they'd be caught between both Philippon and Soult. Everything hinged on those brave souls suffering unimaginable horror. If they failed, everything they'd fought for over the past four years would be undone. The Peninsula, and indeed all of Europe, would be lost.

# Chapter IX: Not Supposed to Succeed
## The Castle, midnight

A Connaught Ranger storming the castle

*"Come on into Badajoz!"*
*"Surely you can try again!"*
*"Come in to Badajoz!"*

The heavily accented cajoling from the French defenders enraged Picton. It was similar to what was happening in the breaches. The defenders were growing more brazen, knowing the British could not possibly get into the city. Badajoz was proving indeed to be impenetrable. Their laughter from the ramparts sickened Picton, as it made a mockery of his fallen. So eager had many of his lads been, that too many piled onto some of the ladders at once, causing them to break. For the poor lads who'd been near the top, the results were fatal. French gunfire hammered them as they tried again and again to carry the castle wall.

"Frog bastards," Picton swore as he walked over to where a regiment was making ready to attack the wall again. *"With me!"* As he started up the ladder, a musket ball bounced off a rock and slammed into the general's groin. He fell from the ladder and landing on his feet, used his sword to hold himself upright.

One of his officer's eyes grew wide, as he'd seen Picton hit. "Sir, are you alright?" Picton, though unable to speak, held up a hand, keeping the officer at bay. He started to swoon and continued to use his sword to prop himself up. His vision was blurred and his mind tormented with pain, yet he refused to fall. He felt his groin with his free hand, and though the injury was terribly painful, he could not feel any blood… a good sign. Still, for the moment he was incapacitated, and it would have been a simple task for a French defender to pick him off. Had he been wearing his conspicuous general's uniform, doubtless one of them would have.

For Lieutenant James Webster, he wondered how much longer he needed to be tormented before death came for him. The continuous concussion of cannon blasts had left his body trembling and numb. His wounded legs had bled profusely, though he was still oblivious to the injuries, and thankfully the blood clotted. He could scarcely hear anymore, all he could do was feel the wall of sound as it assailed him time and again. Lying next to him, Sergeant Davis looked worn and defeated. He had promised not to willingly die before they'd taken the breach, and yet here they were, stuck where they'd been two hours before. James could no longer hear Shanahan's curses; though whether this was because of the assault his hearing had taken or the Irish corporal had been killed was unknown. The soldier from his company who'd bet on the Forlorn Hope being wiped out before the first wave attacked now lay sprawled on his back. Blood dripped from his forehead. James could not tell if the man was dead or simply knocked senseless. He thought he could see the soldier's chest rising and falling, yet with the unending blasts of cannon rocking the earth, it was impossible to know for certain.

All units had committed to battle, there were no more waves to try and take the breach. What was happening, both at the Trinidad and Santa Maria bastions, were officers and non-commissioned officers rallying groups of men to try and crack the enemy's defences. They were valiant, albeit futile gestures. There was no room for manoeuvre in the ditches or on the slopes leading into the breaches, so rallying had to be done on the British side of the line. This meant those returning to the assault had to go back through the killing fields in front of, in, and on the far side of the ditches. The attacks had lost all momentum, and while Lieutenant Webster and Sergeant Davis contemplated when would be a good time to throw themselves in front of a cannon or onto a *chevaux de frise*, the spent survivors of the 4th and Light Divisions were catching their breath and wondering if there was any point in going back.

Twenty agonizing minutes had passed, but now the pain had lessoned to the point that Picton could reasonably function again. He saw his men starting to break under the barrage of French fire and insults from above. He gritted his teeth and rushed back into the fray.

*"Bastards of the Fighting 3rd!"* he shouted, "you have never failed before, do not disgrace the King's uniform now! This division has never lost a battle, and if we cannot take the castle, then let us die upon its walls! Come, who will die with me?"

The unloved but much respected general, in that moment, reinvigorated his men. Many had seen him injured, and now he not only was encouraging them to attack once more, he was offering to die at their side. He then saw Lieutenant Mackie running towards his position.

"Sir, Colonel Ridge has found a place on the wall our ladders can scale!" he shouted. "It's off to the right; he's leading the 5th Foot up there now!"

"Well then, come on, man, let's join him!" Picton replied with renewed enthusiasm. He then directed the nearest regimental commander to give them covering fire as he hobbled after the young officer through the mass of men who were launching yet another assault on the impenetrable walls.

There was indeed a point on the wall that was noticeably lower than the rest of the rampart. How it had been missed baffled Picton. It did not matter. What mattered was that Colonel Henry Ridge was leading his men up one of the ladders; French defenders on top attempting, in vain, to overturn it. The general watched as Lieutenant Mackie started up the ladder to the left of the colonel. As he finally saw British redcoats clamber over the walls, Picton let a rare smile cross his face; the pain in his groin temporarily forgotten. He knew there was no stopping his men now.

"Send word to Wellington immediately," he informed an aide. Despite the agonizing pain in his groin, he gritted his teeth and started up the ladder.

Officers, wanting to set the proper example to their men, were among the first over the wall. Rage filled Lieutenant Mackie, and as he clambered over the rampart he grabbed the first Frenchman he saw, who was aiming his musket over the wall and oblivious to his presence. He clutched the man by the throat and slammed him to the ground. With unbridled hatred, he sliced his sword across the hapless defender's throat, leaving him gasping and clutching at his neck as blood gushed from his severed windpipe. Along with Colonel Ridge and a Lieutenant named Macpherson, they stormed along the rampart, slashing their way through French defenders as it was suddenly swarming with British soldiers. As Philippon had concentrated the weight of his defences on the breach, there were insufficient numbers of French soldiers to hold the castle. As Colonel Ridge drove his sword beneath the ribcage of one soldier, Mackie grabbed the man nearest him by the groin and with maddening strength, threw him screaming over the wall.

The situation grew more desperate for the defenders as they became aware of the number of redcoats storming over the ramparts. A Frenchman turned quickly and fired his musket into Macpherson, who fell into Mackie. A private of the 5th Foot Guards was quickly over the side, and he bayoneted the man in the stomach, dropping him to his knees in indescribable pain. Two other men stabbed the dying man repeatedly, his cries for mercy unheeded. The French taunts were replaced by cries of fear as British soldiers surged in an unstoppable tide of fury.

"Oh shit, that hurts!" Macpherson grunted as he clutched his chest. There was clearly a hole in his frock coat, yet no blood.

"Hurts nothing, you should be dead, sir," Mackie noted in astonishment.

His fellow lieutenant then reached into his breast pocket and pulled out a Spanish dollar with a deep dent in the centre. "Well, I'll be buggered." He then looked over to where the French flag flew from the castle's flagstaff. "Be a good fellow and wait for me, I'll be right back."

# Chapter X: Rest, Soldier, Rest

Fitzroy James Henry Somerset

*"Where the bloody hell is Wellington?"* the messenger shouted frantically from atop his horse.

"Damn your impudent tongue!" Wellington retorted. "Who wants to know?"

"Lieutenant Tyler, Picton's aide de camp," the man replied. "Apologies, my lord."

"Well out with it, man!" Wellington snapped. He was already at his wit's end, and the last thing he needed was yet another report telling him that more of his men were falling valiantly and needlessly.

"General Picton's compliments, sir. He wishes to inform your grace that he's taken the castle."

Wellington closed his eyes and breathed deeply through his nose as an immeasurable wave of relief washed over him.

"If Picton has taken the castle," he noted, "then the town is ours."

"That it is, sir," his aide, Lord Fitzroy Somerset replied with his own immense sense of relief. "Looks like Picton may win his wager after all."

Just then, another messenger rode up from the opposite direction.

"Sir, compliments of General Leith," the man said excitedly. "He says to inform your grace that the 5$^{th}$ Division has taken the San Vincente bastion and is advancing into the town!"

Wellington nodded, the air of disaster and misfortune now turning from relief to triumph. He turned to his aide. "Somerset, what is the disposition of the 4$^{th}$ and Light Divisions?"

"As you'd ordered, sir, they've retired to their battle lines," Somerset replied.

"I need you to implore them to go into the breaches one last time," Wellington replied. "If we are to complete our victory, they must finish what they've started."

"Very good, my lord."

Somerset quickly rode to where Lowry Cole was rallying his exhausted division. A further ways down the line, Alten was doing the same with the Light Division. The commander of the 4$^{th}$ was a fearful sight; his eyes were bloodshot, face covered in soot and numerous cuts, his normally immaculate uniform shredded and burned. There was no semblance of order amongst the men. Many sat or lay on the ground, trying desperately to catch their breath, bodies and souls in shock from the hellish torment they'd endured. Some had passed out completely and lay prostrate upon the sodden earth. Even the officers and non-commissioned officers lay in heaps, unwilling or unable to try and organize their men.

In the darkness, and given Lowry Cole's fearful sight, Somerset did not even notice him, but instead rode up to another officer named Harry Smith.

"Mister Smith," Somerset said, "Wellington's compliments on the courage and tenacity of your men. He implores you to storm the breach once more."

"Like bloody hell!" Smith retorted. "Look at my men. If we were not able to take the breaches when we were fresh, what makes Wellington think we have a chance of taking them now?" He then paused and took a deep breath, lowering and shaking his head in resignation. An order from Wellington, no matter how futile it seemed, was not to be ignored. "Likely we'll make a poor showing, but let his grace know we will try again."

"It may please you to know that General Picton has taken the castle," Somerset explained.

The defeated expression changed to one of astonishment on both Smith and Lowry Cole's faces.

"Tell Wellington we will take the breaches at once!" Lowry Cole stated, startling Somerset, who until this time had not recognized the general.

"By your leave, sir!" Somerset replied with a sharp salute.

*"Men of the 4th Division!"* Smith shouted, eliciting weakened gazes from his shattered men. *"The castle has fallen, and Wellington implores us to assault once more! Will we allow the bastards of the Fighting 3rd to beat us into Badajoz?"*

*"No!"* a private roared as he struggled to his feet.

"Well spoken, Mister Smith," Cole said, giving the young officer a friendly pat on the shoulder as men renewed their battle cries and started to form for yet another assault.

"Apologies, sir," Smith replied. "Excitement got the best of me; I did not mean to speak in your place."

"No harm done," the general replied. "What say we lead these men into Badajoz? And if, by God, we cannot carry the breach this time, I'll let the frogs break every bone in my body."

James was in a battered stupor when he noticed an unusual calm he thought he'd never feel again. He looked around and noted the enemy cannon and gunfire had stopped. The smoke was starting to dissipate a little, and he dared to poke his head up from behind the rock. Remarkably, no shots came his way.

"Here, Thomas!" he shouted, nudging the dazed sergeant. "The enemy guns have stopped!"

"So I just noticed," Thomas replied. "Bastards are still ringing in me ears, though."

*"I'll be buggered!"* a voice shouted to their right. It was Corporal Shanahan, who was standing and pointing excitedly towards the castle. "Sir, look!"

In the soft glow of light that came up from Badajoz, they could just see the flagstaff. The French tricolour was gone. In its place was

76

a British officer's red frockcoat. He then noted that the soldier from his company with the bleeding forehead had recovered enough to regain consciousness.

"Sir, listen," the soldier said.

Despite the dull ringing in his ears, James was able to make out the telltale bugle calls sounding the advance. His face fell into a tired smile as he could just make out the sounds of men shouting battle cries and advancing once again. As the 4th Division made its way into the ditch one last time, James stood and almost fell over.

"Bloody hell, sir, when did you get hit?" Sergeant Davis' question caused him to glance down. His legs were peppered with shrapnel tears, and his trousers were soaked in blood mixed with mud and grime.

"Bloody hell, I didn't know I was," he replied, mimicking the sergeant's profanity. There was no pain yet, though his legs were very stiff. He then looked around and tried to see if any still lived in the carnage of the breach.

*"Brave heroes of the Forlorn Hope and the 4th Division,"* he shouted. *"You have endured the cauldron of hell itself. Whether death takes us this night, know that they cannot hurt you anymore. Who will come with me into Badajoz?"*

Gerard had noticed the falling of the French flag even before the British survivors in the breach. The red frockcoat seemed to mock him; where moments before he had been relishing in triumph, now all was lost. The number of troops storming the castle alone had the Badajoz garrison outnumbered. And like the crack that told of the breaking of a dam, soon the defences would be shattered in a wave of Wellington's army.

The colonel took a deep breath and fought to find his resolve. If he could divert enough men to the castle and still hold the breach, perhaps they could repel this attack; though how the British had even gotten over the walls of the castle perplexed him. He then hoped that the San Vincente bastion had not fallen as well. Quickly he grabbed one of his majors by the shoulder, and pointed to the flagpole. The man's eyes grew wide.

"It cannot be!" the major lamented. "How..."

"It doesn't matter how!" Gerard snapped. "Go with your men and retake the castle! I will keep the remainder of the battalion here and hold down the breach."

"Sir," the major said before shouting a series of orders to the men on the rampart. The commotion caused a stir, and suddenly, every French defender within Badajoz seemed to notice the flagpole at once. Panic struck them, where moments before they had been laughing and hurling insults at the hapless British attackers stuck in the breaches. As Gerard looked off to his right, he saw numerous soldiers rushing from the Santa Maria bastion towards the San Vincente, and he surmised that it had fallen as well.

*"Stand your ground!"* he shouted to the remaining defenders on the rampart, though terror had already started to grip them. Suddenly, a volley of British gunfire erupted from the breach, tearing into them. Several fell screaming to the ground and a round struck Gerard in the shoulder. As he dropped to a knee and clutched the bleeding wound, it baffled him that any of their enemies were still alive and able to fight. It was then that Gerard heard the sounds of trumpets, and his instincts told him this next assault could not be held.

There were more shouts and battle cries coming from the frightful scene than James could have imagined. Though most of the poor souls still on the slope had already passed into eternity, a number of men were struggling to their feet. Many were propped up by their companions, and all eager to continue the fight. The lieutenant and the sergeant started to negotiate their way through the *chevaux de frise*. Had the castle not fallen and drawn away the defenders, they never would have gotten through the breach. Some returning soldiers brought pickaxes with which to smash the chains holding the hated obstacles in place.

As they crawled over the rampart they noted a handful of fallen French soldiers, many of whom had been shot in the face and head. One poor fellow was on his stomach, trying to crawl away. James let go of Sergeant Davis and hobbled over to the man, who looked up at him pleadingly. It was then that the horrors of the assault and the suffering inflicted on his men turned James' soul to ice. He swung his sword down as hard as he could, the blade tearing into the back of the man's neck, severing his spinal column. The hapless Frenchman gave a look of terrible pain, biting hard into his protruding tongue, before mercifully expiring. James wrenched his sword free and turned back to Sergeant Davis. The man who he'd only known for the past two days, who'd loyally fought as his second through the hell of the Trinidad bastion, looked rather serene in sharp comparison to the chaos around them. James' eyes grew wide in realization.

"It is time," Davis said contentedly. "I said I'd follow you into the breach, and here we are." He then turned and faced a group of French defenders who were reforming and started to calmly walk towards them.

British soldiers were pouring into the town, and a brawl ensued between them and the now-desperate defenders.

James limped as quickly as he was able towards the sergeant. His legs still refused to function properly. A French soldier raised his weapon to fire, but the musket failed to discharge. Sergeant Davis threw down his rifle and held his hands out from his sides. The Frenchman grinned sinisterly and stabbed him beneath the ribcage with his bayonet.

"No!" James screamed as he stumbled over to his sergeant, who was now down on his knees, the Frenchman grinding the bayonet into him with a look of glee. His expression turned to horror as James raised his pistol into his face. The man wrenched his weapon free, but the dying sergeant grabbed him by the jacket with the last of his strength, preventing him from bringing his weapon up to defend himself. James then placed the muzzle of his pistol between the Frenchman's eyes and fired. The man's head exploded in a spray of scorched flesh, skull fragments, and brain matter that covered the lieutenant.

James dropped to his knees as Davis let the dead Frenchman fall with a sickening thud onto the cobblestones. The sergeant fell back into his arms, and despite the growing pain in his legs, James held the man close, trying to comfort him in his last moments.

"Christ almighty, this hurts!" Sergeant Davis grimaced. "Bastard could have at least had the decency to properly maintain his weapon and shoot me through the heart!"

James had no words. What could he tell a man who wanted to die? For a moment, the spectre of fury coming through the breaches was lost to him. In the storm of ongoing battle, he briefly felt the sense of peace that Thomas Davis was now succumbing to.

The sergeant's eyes grew wide for a second, and he looked up at his officer. "Sir," he said, grabbing James by the sleeve of his tattered frockcoat, "do me a favour…tell me sons that I fought well. And in return…I'll send your love to your wife, except you never told me her name."

"Her name is Amy," James said, tears rolling down his face.

"Amy," Davis noted. "Same name as your beautiful daughter. Fitting that is…" With a final breath, his grip slackened, and Sergeant Thomas Davis passed into eternity.

"Rest, soldier, rest," James said quietly as he laid the man down and struggled to get to his feet. Unbeknownst to him, the scabbing over the wounds to his legs tore and they now bled afresh.

## Chapter XI: Unholy Vengeance

Despite his ever-stoic appearance, Wellington was torn with a hundred conflicting emotions. He was immensely relieved the town had fallen, and he no longer needed to worry about being trapped between two French armies and losing everything he'd fought for. At the same time, the reports of so many brave men lost wrenched at him. Whatever he may have thought of the common British soldier, each man lost in the breaches and on the walls of Badajoz had performed heroically. Due to the fearful nature of their losses, the latest reports Wellington was receiving most disturbed him.

"Sir," a rider said as he rode up and saluted. "It is chaos within the city."

"A battle is always chaos," Wellington replied dismissively.

"No, sir," the man replied. "It is not the chaos of battle. It is what the men are now doing within the city. They are blood-lusted beyond measure. The hounds of hell have been unleashed, and they wear red coats."

Wellington closed his eyes and shook his head sadly. Despite his best efforts to reign in the savage instincts of his men, he could not possibly hope to do so in light of what they had been through. Doubtless his men were now falling upon the hapless citizens of Badajoz, fuelling their rage with drink and unholy vengeance.

"It was unavoidable," he lamented quietly.

As Wellington sat astride his horse, brooding, Somerset rode up to him.

"Your grace!" he said excitedly. "Baron Philippon has been captured!"

"The devil, you say," Wellington replied, though his expression remained unchanged.

"It's true," Somerset explained. "Once the castle was taken, he took the bridge over to our lines and promptly surrendered. A number of the French garrison have done the same."

"Then only the city itself can bear the wrath of what we have unleashed," Wellington said quietly.

Gerard's men broke and started to flee as British soldiers poured through the breach. A captain with a badly wounded arm and noticeable limp was forming his men into a firing line. He raised his sword up, and they aimed their weapons towards Gerard and what was left of his men. He closed his eyes as the British officer shouted an order that was quickly drowned out by the wall of gunfire. Several musket balls tore into the French colonel; one struck him through the left lung, another smashed into his groin, one shattered his left kneecap, and still another struck him in the shoulder. He fell to the ground, writhing in pain. A subsequent battle cry erupted from the attackers, and they charged with the bayonet. Their fury could not be contained, and even those who tried to surrender were killed without mercy. One soldier stood over Gerard and made ready to stab him. Then, seeing that the colonel was fatally stricken, the soldier instead spat on him and joined his companions in the rampage.

As he lay breathing his last, Gerard lamented not for himself but for his wife. The wave of vengeance that spilled into the city would not be satisfied with the slaying of the French garrison. The dying colonel prayed that if she were to die, Déjà be spared the torments that were sure to be set upon the rest of the women within Badajoz.

In another part of the city, the 3$^{rd}$ Division made good on its bet to be first into Badajoz, and with no more French soldiers to kill, they turned on the populace. Having taken part in the assault of the castle and seeing firsthand what it cost his men, Picton was almost indifferent to the maddened beasts they had become. The French defenders on the ramparts had been slaughtered without mercy, for they had shown none during the attack. As he made his way into the town, he noted a group of Connaught Rangers smashing down the door of a house. They quickly emerged with all manner of plunder. With them was Lieutenant Mackie, who was slashing away at a helpless French soldier with maddened ferocity. Though looting had been expressly forbidden, even the officers who'd once threatened to hang those who committed atrocities upon the people of Badajoz, were now taking part in them. Once he ceased in his screams and thrashing, Mackie turned and stood defiantly in front of his commanding general.

"General, sir," he said. "Are we now to be called the *Connaught Robbers?*"

Picton looked over at the group of men. Their faces were covered in soot, blood, and grime. Their uniforms scorched, torn, and soiled. They were a fearful sight, straight from the bowels of hell. Their rage at the loss of their friends could only be quenched in the bloodlust of revenge, and Picton was not about to stop them.

"No," he replied with a shake of his head. "You are now the Connaught *Heroes*. Carry on, Captain Mackie."

James Webster was not so casual in his observance of his comrades' actions. The defeat of the French garrison in all its brutality he could understand, yet he could not fathom what was now happening to his men, who just a short time before had conducted themselves with complete dignity and valour. Bloodlust and vengeance had changed them into something terrible. The streets were filled with redcoats, and they were in a collective berserker rage.

Leaning against a post outside of a house was the man from his company with the bleeding forehead. He held a cup in his hand, which he greedily drank from as his fellows stormed into the house, gleefully smashing through the door and laughing in spite of the screams that came from within.

"Lieutenant, sir," the soldier said, raising his cup in salute as James hobbled over to him. The boyish playfulness in the man's eyes was gone. They were red, distant. James could sense the burning hatred behind them.

"What have you got there?" James asked, unsure as to what else to say.

"Finest Spanish vintage, sir!" the soldier slurred, thrusting the cup towards him. "Here, have a drink with me. Let us who are damned indulge ourselves in this hour of our revenge."

James did not know what else to do, so he took the cup from the man and drank greedily. His mouth was completely parched, and the sweet-tasting wine felt good running down his throat. He completely finished the cup, eliciting a cheer from the soldier.

"That's right, sir!" the man said with a laugh, smacking James on the shoulder.

As James threw the cup onto the ground, he noted the sudden change in the soldier's demeanour.

His eyes grew dark, and the smile left his face. His mouth was twitching, with a stream of wine and slobber running down the corners of his mouth like a rabid dog. "And now, sir," the man said, his voice shaking, "Time for me to avenge our lads." His face twisted into a sneer of rage as he grabbed his musket and stormed into the house with a howl of unbridled fury.

James was still in a stupor, and the Spanish wine he'd ingested was not helping his judgment. He knew Wellington's orders regarding looting, but as he looked around, it seemed as if the entire army had gone completely mad. People who fled from their homes were beaten or shot, with any women being drug off to be defiled.

As he stumbled down the road, James watched in horror as men smashed in the door to a nunnery. When one of the sisters stood defiantly in the doorway, a soldier shot her in the stomach at close range. James then hobbled over to the entrance as soldiers rushed frantically past him on either side. The French garrison were mostly either slain or run off. There was no one except the citizens of Badajoz for the British army to exact its revenge upon.

At the door to the nunnery, the woman who'd tried to prevent the soldiers from entering lay in a pool of blood and bodily fluids. Her body twitched weakly as death took her. James stepped inside and immediately regretted doing so. Musket shots rang out from inside. A French soldier was curled up in the corner, where a pair of redcoats smashed his brains in with the butts of their weapons. A nun screamed as she was punched in the stomach, bent over a table, and forcibly raped by a young soldier as his companions cheered him on. The shrieks of women coming from the upper floors told of similar acts happening to every hapless woman within the nunnery.

*"What are you doing?"* James shouted at the men.

They either ignored him or simply stared at him dumbfounded.

"By God, this is a holy place! What the *fuck* do you think you are doing?"

84

"Exacting our revenge," a soldier spat contemptuously. "And I wouldn't worry too much about God. Clearly He has abandoned this place!"

A corporal then calmly walked over to him. The man was the only non-commissioned officer James could see in the chaos of men and the cries of hapless women.

"Don't try to stop them, sir," the corporal said quietly. The man's face was bloodied and his uniform tattered and burned in numerous places. His breath was rank with gin, and his eyes glazed in a combination of alcohol, numbing shock, and utter exhaustion.

"And what will you do, corporal?" James asked, his eyes wet with sorrow. To have survived the hell storm of the last few hours, only to see that his fellow soldiers had become hell spawn themselves tore into his very soul.

"Me?" the corporal asked with a snort. He then took a swig of gin before answering. "I lost a dozen men in that fucking breach. Many more are missing arms and legs, and others with their guts torn out are even now crying out to God to end their pain. The lads are right, sir; God has abandoned this place. So what will I do, you ask? I will have my revenge. You do not have to join us, sir, but do not try and stop us. No one can save us now."

Shamed as he was by the men's conduct, James knew the corporal was right. Their madness, which was now being supplemented by looted drink, would overwhelm any sense of decency they had. There was no officer who could stop it now, not even Wellington.

The screams of women pierced the din of the rampage, and were followed with raucous laughter of the triumphant conquerors. James suddenly felt light-headed and he stumbled out the door. He took a number of deep breaths, but could not seem to clear his head. At first he thought it was effects of the Spanish wine, but then became aware of the severity of his wounds. His once-white trousers were now caked in mud, grime, and completely saturated in blood. It was not just exhaustion that was overwhelming him; the loss of blood was far worse than he realized. As he started to fade, he no longer cared about the chaos around him. God would either damn them or not. Perhaps in the cauldron of the breaches, they had already paid the penance for their vile atrocities.

"Sir!" a familiar voice shouted as he started to collapse.

He fell into the arms of the man who shouted to him. As he sank to the ground, James looked up and was glad to see it was Corporal Shanahan.

"What's happened?" James asked weakly. "What is this hell we have unleashed?"

"I'm afraid, sir," the corporal replied, "this is what glorious victory looks like."

Déjà would not be spared from the storm of vengeance. The sounds of screams and battle cries echoed through the nunnery as she and one of the sisters raced into a back bedroom. They attempted to brace the door, but it was quickly smashed in and a pair of half-mad redcoats stormed in. They were both very young and looked more like schoolboys than soldiers. Only the blinding rage radiating from their bloodshot eyes gave away their intentions.

"Well, what have we there then," one sneered as he turned to his companion. "Looky here, this one isn't even a nun or a Spaniard!"

"Pretty that," the other lad said, grinning sinisterly.

*"You will not violate the colonel's wife!"* the nun shouted as she threw herself at the men.

The first soldier burst into laughter as he violently tossed the woman aside, slamming her into the wall by the door.

"Here, you can have that one," the first soldier said to his friend. "The colonel's wife is mine. Nothing like fucking the wife of a frog officer!"

Déjà was gripped with fear as the soldier's eyes filled with lust, and he sinisterly licked his lips.

"I daresay your lovey husband cost me many friends this night," the man said through gritted teeth as he stalked towards Déjà, still brandishing his musket and daring her to try and stop him. "I think it only fitting I take something of his!"

The nun, having recovered from being slammed into the wall, gave an angry shout and jumped onto the man's back, causing his friend to break into a fit of laughter.

"What the bloody piss!" the first soldier shouted as he viciously threw the nun back into the wall. Before she could react, he quickly raised his weapon and fired into her face, the back of her head exploding into the wall.

"Bugger that," the second soldier muttered, suddenly in shock.

*"No!"* Déjà screamed as the maddened soldier turned and slammed the butt of his musket into her stomach. Her breath was taken from her, and she doubled over.

The man then grabbed her by the hair and threw her violently onto the bed. Scarcely able to breathe, she fought in vain against his animal lust as he savagely violated her.

For the soldier, it wasn't about sexual gratification. Driven into the abyss of insanity, this was about revenge. The unleashing torrent of unholy lust was a way of gaining retribution for all the suffering and pain inflicted upon them in the hellish breaches. The survivors would later reason that if Philippon had only been decent enough to surrender beforehand, all the needless suffering of the populace could have been avoided. As it was, not knowing whether her husband was already dead, Déjà Aubert, like so many others within Badajoz, bore the brunt of the British soldiers' vengeance. Her screams ceased after the first minute, and the only sound was the man's fierce grunting and the slamming of the bed against the wall. Once the soldier finished, he stood over her, red-faced and eyes clouded.

"Please..." she sobbed, drowned as she was in her own sorrow. "Please kill me...torment me no longer."

"Very well, love," the soldier replied coldly. His face expressionless, he retrieved his weapon and slammed the bayonet through her heart. Déjà's eyes grew wide for a brief moment before death took her.

Corporal Shanahan struggled with the weight of the unconscious Lieutenant Webster draped across his back. All around him was the wild chaos of an army gone mad. The Irish corporal neither condoned nor condemned them for their conduct. No one could have survived the torments they had without being driven temporarily insane. He was thankful his sense of duty in saving the life of his lieutenant gave him a reprieve from his own bloodlust.

"Here, that's my officer!" a voice shouted.

Patrick turned and saw it was the same soldier from Lieutenant Webster's company who'd fought beside them in the breach.

The man stumbled towards them, his expression one of both shock and rage. "Bloody frogs got him!"

"He's not dead, you drunken sod!" Patrick rebuked the man. "But he will be dead if I don't get him to hospital soon."

"Well, I know what I must do then," the soldier replied.

As Patrick walked away, the sounds of a woman's screams alerted him. He saw the soldier dragging a young French woman by the hair. She was scarcely able to stand as he dragged her along the cobblestones, her face covered in cuts and bruises.

*"You see this?"* the soldier screamed at her. "You bloody frogs did this to him and to me friends!"

"Damn it, man!" Patrick barked. "What do you think you're doing?"

"Exacting retribution for my officer," the soldier replied through gritted teeth, "and letting this little bitch know *why* she is about to become my little plaything."

The woman started to cry out in protest once more, only to be silenced when the soldier punched her in the stomach.

"One more thing, corporal," the soldier said with a brief trace of sanity and sadness in his eyes. "Thank you for saving our officer. Do yourself a favour and do not return to this place, lest your soul become lost with the rest of us."

# Chapter XII: Victory Drowned in Sorrow and Rage
## Santa Maria bastion, Badajoz
## 7 April 1812, morning

Like the rest of the army, Wellington had not slept since the day before. He was drained and distraught over the more graphic reports coming from inside Badajoz. As the sun rose, he decided to see the chaos for himself. As he, Somerset, and others of his staff rode through the streets, he was appalled by the complete lack of discipline from his army. It seemed every building was occupied by drunken redcoats, who having plundered what they could carry, were smashing whatever remained, while taking their turns on the hapless women of the city.

"Scum of the earth," he muttered under his breath.

Any outrages he may have harboured were quickly tempered as he dismounted his horse and walked through the Santa Maria breach. The bodies of the dead lay strewn in front of the trench. A few wounded struggled to crawl away, many with wounds so fearful that death would be a mercy. After many such horrific battles, there were always numbers of civilians amongst the dead, plundering as much as they could before being driven off. It was commonly accepted that the living should make use of what the dead could no longer, and soldiers would often plunder even from their closest friends who had perished. Yet for the civilians within Badajoz, they were trapped and at the mercy of the British army. Wellington could hear the madness coming from within; a horrifying amalgamation of women's screams, men howling in rage, and even occasional musket fire.

Despite the untold outrages being committed by his troops, all Wellington could focus on was the scene of death. Hundreds of bodies lay sprawled along the slope that led into the breach. Amongst the slain he noted the torn body of Lieutenant Benedict Harvest, who had led the Light Division's Forlorn Hope. His throat was ripped open and soaked in coagulated crimson. His left arm was completely torn off, and his guts were strewn out several feet from his body. Wellington knelt and placed a hand on the young man's shoulder and bowed his head. He almost never showed emotion; even his wife had always found him to be cold and distant. And yet, seeing so many lives shattered in what had been truly a forlorn action, he was overwhelmed. So many had died, and he was consumed with guilt thinking many died needlessly. Lieutenant Harvest had easily been young enough to be Wellington's son, as were many of the lads who fell in that awful breach.

For once, Wellington's stoicism failed him, and he placed a hand over his eyes and openly wept. It was then that he understood the fury with which the survivors were now savaging Badajoz. Such acts would be forever burned into infamy, but then, historians would never have to look upon the awful carnage those men had endured.

As Wellington lost control of his emotions, his aides kept a respectful distance. They, too, were horrified and saddened by the sight within the breach. Most of them had lost comrades and cursed themselves for not taking part in the assault; though from what they could tell from the abject sight of death, they would have done their friends little good. One man who seemed baffled by Wellington's rare show of emotion was General Picton. He was still limping; the pain of his wound returning, and perhaps preventing him from understanding his commanding officer's sorrow.

"Good God, man, what is the matter?" Picton asked, his crassness perhaps understandable, given his painful state.

Wellington did his best to compose himself and stood to face Picton. His eyes were swollen and his cheeks red. Tears stained both sides of his face.

After a minute, his provost marshal walked over to him, his expression one of concern. "My lord, my provosts are ready to carry out your orders to execute any man caught in the act of looting, except…well, there are so many who are blatantly in the act, even amongst the officers!"

"Let them plunder!" Picton snapped. "Had your provosts gone through this shit, they'd be doing the same, as would you!"

The provost swallowed hard at Picton's biting rebuke, and then turned to Wellington, who had remained silent thus far. "My lord, are we to start hanging looters?"

"No," Wellington finally replied. "Erect a gallows in the town square to act as a deterrent. We will flog any man who assaults an officer, but we will not hang anyone. If God sees fit to damn them, so be it; but I will not."

"Yes, sir," the provost replied with a mixture of resentment at not being allowed to do his job, and at the same time relieved he did not have to try.

As Wellington turned his gaze towards the city, he saw young Harry Smith guiding a pair of women towards them. The younger of the two clung to him protectively. Her dress was torn and her neck covered in blood.

"Your grace," Smith said as he approached Wellington. "This young woman and her mother beseech us for protection."

"Many will seek protection from the rampage we have unleashed," Picton muttered, grimacing once more and clutching at his injured groin.

"What is her name?" Wellington asked Smith; ignoring Picton for the moment.

"Her name is Juana," Smith replied. "And with your grace's permission, I wish to take her as my bride."

"I will personally oversee the ceremony," Wellington replied. He then took the bridle of his horse from an aide, mounted, and rode slowly back to the town.

Juana smiled in both relief and joy and kissed Smith passionately. He held her close and took her mother by the hand, guiding them towards the city gates. He saw groups of men firing their weapons in the air and cheering as Wellington rode past them. Despite the ravages they were committing on the populace, even the most enraged and drunken soldiers would not dare assault a woman under the personal protection of an officer.

The rest of the day passed with the continued looting and destruction from within Badajoz. Wellington determined it would eventually burn out on its own accord. Back at the hospital tents, throughout the day and into the following night, a young officer lay unconscious, an Irish corporal ever by his side.

*"Lieutenant Webster?"* the voice echoed in James' mind as he slowly regained consciousness. His vision was clouded, his mouth completely parched, and he felt like he was burning up. His legs were completely numb, and he started slapping them erratically to

make certain they had not been amputated. A pair of hands grabbed a hold of his shoulders, and he immediately felt exhausted. As his vision cleared, he saw it was Corporal Shanahan who had a grip on him.

"There he is now," the Irishman said happily. "You still with us, sir?"

"Patrick," James replied, calling the corporal by his given name for the first time.

"Aye, sir, I haven't left your side," Shanahan explained. "Can't have the only bloody officer to survive the Forlorn Hope die on us now that the battle is over."

"How…how did I end up here?"

"The good corporal carried you, all the way from the bastion," the surgeon explained as he knelt and placed a damp cloth on the lieutenant's head.

"How long have I been here?" James asked. He had lost all sense of time and did not know if hours had passed or days.

"Two days, it is now the 8th of April," the surgeon answered as he turned and left to check on other patients. The hospital tent was full of badly maimed soldiers, many of whom cried piteously from the awful pain of their injuries.

"Thought we were going to lose you there for a while," Shanahan said. "You became sick from loss of blood; the clotted wounds on your legs reopening when we entered the town. You were so numb; you probably didn't feel a thing."

"I didn't," James agreed. "The last I remember was feeling like I'd stepped from one nightmare into another. Our own soldiers, they'd gone completely mad!"

"And it hasn't stopped," Shanahan added sadly. "Nothing has been able to stop their bloodlust, not even Wellington. The provosts erected a gallows in the square, and a handful of lads have been flogged for lashing out against their own officers, but no one's been done in for the crimes that continue in Badajoz. I think Old Nosey is just letting it end on its own. He curses the lads for their offenses, yet praises their sacrifice and bravery. An awful conundrum from a terrible situation all around."

"Sad," James remarked. He thought for a minute and then recalled the men he'd led. "Any of the other lads survive, or are you and I all that's left of the Forlorn Hope?"

"Private Lawrence made it," Shanahan answered, "somehow managed to get all the way back to our lines. Wellington's own surgeon saw to him. I managed to find an additional six survivors, though I pray there are others. To be honest, sir, I cannot tell for certain. I didn't have time to get to know the lads any more than you did." He smiled sadly at his last remark.

Just then, the flap of the tent was thrown back by a guard, and Wellington himself walked in. His face was pale, and James wondered if he'd gotten any sleep over the last few days. Corporal Shanahan immediately stood and backed away. Wellington did not seem to notice him.

"Lieutenant Webster, I see you are still with us." His voice was stern, and James could not tell if he was pleased or disappointed that he lived.

"Yes, sir," was all he could reply.

"Good," Wellington replied, though he still did not smile. "Too many good men have died in this hellish siege. Our officer ranks have especially been depleted. Your regiment lost its colonel, with both majors wounded. Your own company commander lives, though his arm is in a sling and he can barely walk."

James let the words sink in. To think that his colonel had been more distraught over a young subaltern's decision to volunteer for the Forlorn Hope than he was in his own safety. But then, officers were expected to lead their regiments by their example; a trait that bought many an early death. James would later find out that when the 3$^{rd}$ Division successfully took the castle, the first three men over the wall were a colonel and two lieutenants. An Irish major had been among the first to successfully enter the Santa Maria breach, and he'd paid for it with his life.

As he contemplated the loss of his friends and brothers, James noted Wellington cracking the slightest trace of a smile. It was a sad one, but a smile nonetheless. He reached into his coat and pulled out a single epaulette, which he handed to James.

"See to it you live long enough that you may wear this with honour," he emphasized.

James noted the captain's insignia on the epaulette.

"An honour I hope to live up to, sir," he managed to say.

Wellington nodded in reply and made to leave, stopping himself short at the door.

"One more thing," he said. "You had one non-commissioned officer in the Forlorn Hope that survived, a Corporal Shanahan."

"Here, sir!" the Irish corporal said quickly, snapping his heels together.

Wellington raised an eyebrow at him.

"Do be a good man and report back to your regiment at once," he said sternly. "That is unless you want to remain on the *missing and presumed dead* list, thereby forfeiting your wages."

"Right away, sir!" Shanahan started to exit quickly when Wellington snapped at him.

"I did not say you were dismissed!" he barked. Allowing the corporal a moment's consternation, he then pulled a set of chevrons from his coat and shoved them into the man's chest. "Here, tell your commander these come with my compliments."

Shanahan's eyes grew wide, and he smiled broadly as he eyed the patch bearing three chevrons.

"Much obliged, your grace."

Wellington cracked a rare smile once more. "Dismissed, *sergeant*."

Shanahan quickly left the tent, giving a loud whoop as soon as he was outside. Wellington simply gave a short nod to the newly-promoted captain and left. In an instant, James was left alone. He gave a deep sigh and laid his head back, the draw of sleep coming on, despite it being the middle of the day. This was interrupted once more, though the disturbance was not unwelcome, as it was Captain Daniel Roberts. His face was swollen and red from burns along his left cheek, his left arm in a sling and heavily bound. He did his best to hide his pronounced limp as he took off his hat and greeted his friend.

"Glad to see you made it, old boy," he said with as much enthusiasm as he could in his state of utter exhaustion.

"And to you, sir," James replied.

"Please," Daniel said with a dismissive wave, "a fellow captain is not required to call his peer *sir*." He then took a deep breath, and the feeling of relief that swept over him was apparent. "I do thank God you survived, James."

"And I thank him for keeping you safe, Daniel." It was the first time he'd addressed Captain Roberts by his given name since the latter had taken command of the company. Despite their similarity in

94

age and how close they'd grown over the past three years, he'd never allowed himself to lapse in formality. "How's the arm?"

"It'll mend," Daniel replied. "Legs are a bit stiff, that's because I did take a pretty nasty fall. Burns on my face sting to bloody hell, though. And how about you? You've lost enough blood you could pass for a ghost."

"I admit I don't feel the best," James said while trying to force a smile in vain. "I didn't even know how badly I'd been hit at first."

"Hobbling through the town like you did let plenty of blood flow out of those holes in your legs," Daniel added. "Still, Wellington says you're not allowed to die on us now, especially not after he just made you a captain."

"I am relieved," James said, "but also saddened by what happened to our men. Given the state of madness that gripped the survivors, I can't help but wonder if the dead are the fortunate ones."

"That they may be," Daniel consented. "Still, whatever atrocities the men now commit, it was unavoidable once Philippon decided to try and hold against us. Eventually, all will come to their senses, and the good ones will pray for the rest of their lives that God forgives them for their crimes."

"Do you think He will?" James asked, causing his friend to shrug.

"Thankfully, that's not up to me," he replied. "The forgiveness of God far exceeds that of man; so if even Old Nosey can pardon the men, then perhaps the Almighty can as well. Besides, after what they've been through, it is difficult to condemn them further."

"I wonder then where my next posting will be," James thought aloud, changing the subject.

"Home, for now," Daniel answered. "You've got a long road to recovery, far longer than mine. I'll still at least be able to command the company. I saw General Lowry Cole when I was getting my arm wrapped. He asked how I intend to lead my men, indisposed as I am. I told him an officer only needs one good arm to wield his sword, and if I'm willing to take on the frogs with an arm in a sling and a severe limp, then my lads had better follow me."

James tried to laugh, but it hurt to do so, and he was suddenly feeling delirious. Daniel saw this and clasped his hand comfortingly.

"You rest well now," he said. "We'll see you when you return to us, provided Old Nosey hasn't whipped the frogs all the way back to

Paris by then." As Daniel turned to leave, he stopped himself and reached into his coat. "I almost forgot about this. I took the liberty of securing your belongings and saw the note you left in your chest. Your Bible I left and will have it shipped home with your personal baggage. However, I thought you'd want to keep this with you."

Though James' vision was fading, he felt what he knew to be his locket placed into his hand. Daniel helped him close his fingers around it, before lifting James' hand to his chest and letting it rest there. He was finally able to crack a smile and mouthed the words *thank you* to his friend. He squeezed the locket with the last of his strength and finally allowed himself a feeling of peace as he fell into a deep slumber.

# Chapter XIII: Bittersweet Returns
## Southend-on-Sea, England
### June 1812

The wounds and infections in his legs had left their scars, and James found it difficult to walk, even after two months. At least his fever had finally subsided, though his face was pale, and he still had trouble eating. Such had made his journey back through Portugal tortuous. Any feelings of guilt at leaving his friends who were left to continue the fight were fleeting in wake of his condition. He had not, at first, figured his injuries sustained at Badajoz to be as severe as they were; however, infection combined with loss of blood made him lucky to even be alive. Doctors had wanted to amputate both legs rather than risk gangrene. He protested loudly enough that they refrained.

"Any officer who survives leading the Forlorn Hope," a doctor reasoned, "and is promoted by Wellington himself, gets whatever he wants. I think he's tough enough to stop gangrene from setting in."

There were thousands of other wounded souls invalided back to England, many with missing limbs and other disabilities. James noted the bugler whose advice he had followed to bathe before the assault. The man had survived as part of the Santa Maria Forlorn Hope, though he'd been shot through the hand and would likely never regain use of it. In all, they suffered four thousand casualties in the taking of Badajoz.

It was thoughts such as these that ran through his mind as he exited the carriage that had taken him to the gates of the Webster estate. He had donned a fresh uniform, complete with the captain's epaulette given to him by Wellington. There'd been no way to notify his family, so it was with both trepidation and excitement that, with the use of a cane, he walked through the gate. Having spent time knowing the men in the ranks, he was grateful to have such a home to return to. A wave of happier memories washed over him as he walked up the damp stone path leading to the door. He glanced off to his left and saw a large oak tree that made him smile. It was under its protective shroud that he'd asked his wife to marry him. As a gentle breeze blew through his hair, he could almost hear her voice. He let out a deep sigh and opened the door.

97

As he stepped inside, the tap of his cane gave a loud echo on the hard floor. He stopped and looked around. The house he had grown up in was as it was when he'd left for Portugal, yet it felt foreign to him. It was by no means a mansion; however, it was still far grander than anything his men had to return to, and it certainly did not lack in creature comforts. Straight ahead was the drawing room, with the dining room attached off to its right. To his immediate right were two sets of stairs; one led to the servants' quarters in the basement, and the other led to his family's bedrooms upstairs.

"Young master James!" a voice said excitedly.

James turned to see their elderly butler.

"Hello, Miles," he replied with a smile.

The old man had been a part of his life since the time he was born, and the sight of such a welcome face lifted his spirits as Miles took his hand enthusiastically in his.

"Miles, is there someone at the door?" a woman's voice called from the drawing room.

James turned to his sister, who immediately put her hands over her mouth.

"Hello, Angela," he said with gentle smile.

His sister's eyes filled with tears, and she slowly walked towards him, uncertain if he was really there.

"But..." she stammered as she placed her hands on his shoulders, "how?"

"I was wounded at Badajoz," he explained with an involuntary glance to the floor.

Angela's expression turned to pity for her older brother, and it was then she noted the cane and the limp in his step.

"Beastly affair that was," Miles said quietly.

"We read about it in the papers," Angela added, shaking her head sadly. "So many brave men lost. The bastions were supposed to be the worst; and those poor boys that had to go in first. They called them the *Forlorn Hope*. That name alone rings tragic." James' quick breath alerted her, and she looked him in the eye. "Were you?"

"Forlorn Hope of the Trinidad bastion," he answered with a nod.

Angela then placed her head on his shoulders and embraced him hard.

"But where are mother and father?" James asked as soon as they parted.

98

"Your parents are in Kent for the next fortnight," Miles explained.

James dropped his head in resignation, and then.....the cry of a baby.

"Is that...?" he started to ask.

Angela gave a broad smile and rushed into the drawing room. She returned with a baby girl cradled in her arms. The child was wrapped in a pink woollen blanket and was fussily wiping her eyes. Angela started to hand her to James. He reached for her and then abruptly stopped. He swallowed hard, and a tear came to his eye.

"Where is she?" he asked, looking his sister in the eye. Angela cradled the baby in one arm, while gently guiding her brother by the arm with her free hand.

"I'll take you to her."

James' family had decided not to bury Amy in a public cemetery, but instead gave her a special resting place within their rose garden. The overwhelming fragrance, combined with the warm early summer breeze, contrasted sharply with the smells he had been subjected to over the last four years. He instinctively broke off a single red rose and followed his sister past the hedgerows, climbing vines, and fragrant flower bushes. He thought he had shed all the tears he could for his beloved, but was stricken anew as he cast his gaze on the grave. It was enclosed with a foot-high, stone border, the onyx headstone with white letters stood out against the rose bushes and vines and that adorned it. Angela kept a respectful distance, holding her niece close as James knelt and laid a single rose upon the grave. He placed a hand over his mouth and tears flowed down his cheeks as he looked upon the headstone that read:

Amy Elaine Webster
1788 – 1812
Beloved Wife and Mother
She rests with the Angels

He uttered a few unintelligible words under his breath and hoped God could hear his silent prayer. He prayed for peace in Amy's soul, and that she knew how much he still loved her. Angela waited patiently, giving her brother the time he needed. After a few minutes, he rose and rejoined his sister, who handed his now-sleeping daughter to him. He kissed her forehead and held her close as she slept peacefully in his arms. At that moment, all the love he still harboured for his wife passed on to his daughter. In a sense, through her, his wife still lived. How fitting then, that they shared the same name.

Two more months passed, and with his health rapidly returning, James was anxious to return to Spain and rejoin his regiment. He certainly enjoyed the comforts of home and spent every moment he could with his daughter, who was now crawling and would be walking before long. His time in Portugal and Spain had shown him just how privileged and sheltered his life had been. He thought often about the men who served with him in the 1st Foot Guards, and especially those brave heroes who'd suffered with him as part of the Forlorn Hope at Badajoz. He thought often of the poor bugler from the Light Division's Forlorn. It bothered James that as vivid as his memories were of the man, he never got his name. His own injuries, while briefly life-threatening simply because of the loss of blood and subsequent fever, had mostly healed. That poor bugler had lost use of his hand. He wondered if the man, who had fought with equal bravery, would be able to make a living or was he damned to destitution. And what of those who lost limbs or suffered other disabilities? Would they simply be cast aside by society like broken livestock? One always heard tales of great victories, but never of what became of those who paid the terrible price for those triumphs.

Despite a perpetually unstable home government, opposition to Wellington from certain factions in Parliament along with his constant rivalry with Horse Guards, the newspapers inundated the public with stories of his constant victories as he pushed through Spain. The horrible atrocities committed by the British army at Badajoz were mostly overlooked, with the focus being placed on the heroic sacrifice of so many in the face of insurmountable odds. While this was certainly true, James knew it only told half the story. He then wondered just how much of the horrors of war were kept from the general public? He also realized his own perception was very linear, as he had been focused solely on whatever battle he had been a part of. He noted from the papers that just a few days after Badajoz, a large cavalry force under Sir Rowland Hill's senior cavalry officer, Stapleton Cotton, routed the French cavalry at a place called Villagarcia.

It was now early August and, though word had yet to reach England about Wellington's decisive victory at Salamanca a couple weeks prior, the exploits of the ever-reliable 'Daddy' Hill made the papers. He had led a daring raid on a series of pontoon bridges, catching the French by surprise and completely routing them. It was this raid that kept the French forces separated and unable to mass their superior numbers against the British, and would contribute significantly to Wellington's triumph at Salamanca. Another allied victory happened the day following Salamanca involving British-led German dragoons routing a French army at Garcia Hernandez, inflicting fearful casualties on the French, while suffering minimal losses.

Though he hadn't yet heard of these significant events, James knew that with Ciudad Rodrigo and Badajoz both in British hands, Wellington would now be advancing through Spain, doubtless defeating the French at every turn. It baffled both James and his father, who also kept his eyes fixed on the reports coming out of the Peninsula, that Napoleon still dismissed both Wellington and the British army. Instead of focusing all his attention on the one man who'd repeatedly bested his ablest generals, the French Emperor was, instead, committing all his energies into what would be his grandest folly, the invasion of Russia. Although in the late summer of 1812, with the Russian army constantly beaten and in a series of tactical retreats, it looked as though Napoleon would pull off his greatest triumph. It was apparent that Wellington and his badly outnumbered ragtag army fighting its way through Spain was the only real hope left to save Europe from *the monster*, as Napoleon was often referred.

So it was with much excitement a major from Horse Guards came to the Webster estate. James was now able to walk without the cane, and he was there to greet the man when Miles ushered him into the drawing room.

"Captain Webster?" the major asked.

"Yes, sir," James replied, excitedly taking the man's hand.

101

"Your assignment has been posted," the major said, handing him a sealed envelope, which the young captain greedily tore into.

James' countenance dropped as he read the dispatch inside.

"Sir, there must be some mistake," he pleaded.

"No mistake, sir," the major replied. "You are to report for recruiting duty in two weeks. It's not every day we have a hero who isn't missing limbs, bleeding to death, or gone completely mad. You have the patronage of Wellington, which may wield you extraordinary powers within his army on the continent. However, Horse Guards feels you'd be better suited in charge of finding replacements for Wellington's army, rather than fighting in it."

Every shilling had to be accounted for. The temptation to simply pocket the coin meant to entice new recruits was great. Hence, an officer was responsible for ensuring that every shilling distributed to the recruiting sergeant and his men equalled a new recruit enlisted onto the roles. Though, officially, the army liked to think its best non-commissioned officers and other ranks were used in recruitment, the reality of the time was the best men were all with Wellington in Spain. Instead, the recruiting sergeants were usually older men, with a handful of substandard rankers assigned to assist them. James was very young for a recruiting officer, with most of those chosen being much older and often selected if they had a more genial demeanour that would disarm apprehensive recruits. However, as the major from Horse Guards had told him, he was an ideal choice due to his status as a bona fide hero and survivor of the infamous Forlorn Hope. He would serve as the visual example to the new men who would doubtless be told of his exploits. At the same time, he was responsible for ensuring that the sergeants and men assigned to the *beating order*, as it was called, conducted themselves properly.

It was his first day, and James took stock of his office. It was small, but would suffice for what he needed. He took a seat behind his desk and rolled a coin pouch over in his hand. He had a receipt on his desk, accounting for the currency within the pouch. Once the recruiting sergeant signed for the King's shillings, he was then responsible. Any loss or theft would be on his head. The men assigned to the beating order knew if even one shilling came up missing without a recruit bound to it, it would mean fifty lashes plus loss of rank for any non-commissioned officers responsible. Such stiff penalties ensured that whatever kind of men the local sergeant major assigned to the detail, while *beating up* an area, as it was called, they would be kept honest.

Though James loathed the thought of being stuck on semi-permanent recruiting duty, as opposed to commanding a line company in the Peninsula, the order had come from Horse Guards; the one organization that could trump even Wellington's authority. As he contemplated this, there was a knock at his office door.

"Come!" he ordered, and his sergeant walked in, saluting sharply.

"Sergeant Baker reporting, sir!" the man barked.

"At ease, sergeant," the captain replied. He apprised the man. He was definitely much older, possibly older than James' father. He was balding on top, with sparse traces of gray hairs clinging to his head. He stood erect, trying his best to hide his protruding belly, evidence of life away from the line. Still, his uniform was well-kept, and he carried himself like a professional.

"Your men know the orders?" James asked.

"Yes, sir," the sergeant replied, keeping his eyes straight ahead. "Not my first *beating order*, sir."

James nodded as he tossed the sergeant the pouch of coins. "Here's forty shillings. Return with forty recruits."

"King George commands and we obey, sir," Sergeant Baker said with a grin which James could not help but match.

"Over the hills and far away," he replied.

# Epilogue: Two Years Later

Contemporary depiction of British Foot Guards

*How fitting it is that Napoleon should abdicate on the second anniversary of the Storming of Badajoz. Though ours was but one battle amongst many, Wellington himself said at no point was the army pressed harder than on that horrible night.*

*Wellington, who was recently made a Duke, has asked me to act as one of his escorts to the Congress of Vienna, where the ultimate fate of France, and indeed all of Europe, will be decided. That his entourage is made of some of the most distinguished officers from the Peninsula Campaign, I am deeply honoured to be counted amongst them. It was by a stroke of fortune that amongst the thousands of men converging on Vienna, I happened upon Sergeant Patrick Shanahan, who I had not seen since Badajoz. Though we only knew each other for a couple of days, it was with much joy that we greeted each other. His term of enlistment was set to end, though he told me he would gladly re-enlist, on condition that he serves with me. I was so deeply honoured by his gesture, I assured him I would not only find a place for him, but he should send for his family at once.*

*Word has it a British army will still remain in Belgium. I intend to petition Wellington directly for either a company command or at least a position on his staff. If I can get a company command, that will make it easier for me to find a billet for Sergeant Shanahan, though I don't think I will have much trouble, regardless. On the few occasions I have spent with Wellington, he has always been quick to mention my leading of the Forlorn Hope at Badajoz. Certainly he will find a place for the non-commissioned officer who saved my life that night.*

*My dearest little Amy is with me, for I'll not leave her again. Though I still miss her mother every day, I give her as much love as a father can, and Brussels society will be fitting for her to grow up in. I had the esteemed honour of meeting the Duke and Duchess of Richmond; their own daughters were taken by mine and have promised to care for her like their own sister.*

*As for Bonaparte, he will be left to spend his days on the Isle of Elba with a guard of a thousand men, scarcely the 'Grande Armee' he once commanded. There is talk in many circles about the possibility of his escape and what it could mean if he ever set foot on French soil again. The Bourbon king, Louis XVIII, dismisses such threats as preposterous. As for this humble officer, I think Louis is being naïve and gravely underestimates the infatuation many of his people have for their now-deposed emperor. Such affections baffle me, as he led his nation to ruin after twenty-five years of almost continuous war that left millions dead and even more crippled and impoverished. Perhaps it is the idea of what he represented the French love so much; as even many English, including the Duchess of Richmond, sympathize with his ideals. Personally, I will never understand it. 'The Monster', as many of our lads called him, will always remain a threat as long as he breathes life.*

*I pray to God every day I will not have to draw a blade again in anger nor lead men into the nightmares of death like we endured at Badajoz. I swear I can still hear the cries of the dying and the thunder of cannon and musket, all merged into a symphony of horror. That humanity could ever conceive of inflicting such atrocities upon each other again is unthinkable for reasonable and God-loving men. Yet should the unthinkable happen, and Napoleon returns as the scourge of Europe, I only hope I can stand with Wellington once more.*

*Captain James Henry Webster*
*16 July 1814*

# Historical Notes and Author's Final Thoughts

When I started this project, my focus was on finding a story about a specific event that could serve as a prelude to a future novel. I had originally thought to tell of the Siege of San Sebastian, as it was the last of the Peninsular War. I elected to change this to the Siege of Badajoz after being inspired by the Chris Collingwood painting, *The Storming of Badajoz*, which I obtained permission to use for the cover of this novella.

The other source of inspiration, as well as the main source I used for historical reference, came from Peter Snow's book, *To War with Wellington: from the Peninsula to Waterloo*. His attention to detail is superb, as he uses many direct quotations from both officers and other ranks to paint an accurate picture for the reader of what life must have been like for soldiers serving in Wellington's army. I recommend it for anyone with even a passing interest in the British army of the early 19th Century, as well as that of Wellington himself.

While the character of James Henry Webster is a fictitious one, there are a number of persons in this story who are based on actual people. Many of these came from those quoted by Peter Snow in *To War with Wellington*:

Private William Lawrence was a survivor of the Forlorn Hope from the 40th Regiment, which was part of the 4th Division. The injuries to his legs, deflection of the bullet off his canteen, as well as his trek back to the lines and subsequent interaction with Wellington is all based on actual events.

The hapless bugler, who bathes in the river before the assault and is subsequently shot through the thigh and hand, was based on Bugler William Green, a member of the Light Division's Forlorn Hope. Despite the excruciating pain and his pleading with doctors to amputate his hand, this was refused. The wound to his hand did eventually heal, though he lost effective use of it and was given a very small annuity by the British government in compensation.

Lieutenant William Mackie was a survivor of the Forlorn Hope at Ciudad Rodrigo. Though he should have been rewarded right then, Picton refused to give him his due, since he was with the Connaught Rangers. The dialog between Picton and the Rangers inside Badajoz is true, including his referring to them as the *Connaught Heroes*. It is assumed then, that Mackie would have been given his due, as he had led a Forlorn Hope during one siege and been among the first over the walls of another.

The scene with Lieutenant MacPherson being shot in the chest, only to have the musket ball deflected off a Spanish dollar also actually happened. He soon after ran his coat up the French flagpole to show that the castle had fallen.

Sir Harry and Lady Juana Smith were married three days after the battle, in the presence of Wellington. Despite the hastiness of their decision, Juana accompanied Harry through the rest of the Peninsula War, and they spent a long and happy life together. Harry later served as governor of South Africa, where the cities of Harrismith and Ladysmith are named in their honour.

Lieutenant Benedict Harvest was a semi-composite character, inspired by the young officer shown leading the Light Division's Forlorn Hope in the film *Sharpe's Company*. He states his name is Benedict, but does not give his last name. According to Snow, this officer, who also foreshadowed the end of his luck and subsequent death, was named Lieutenant Harvest. His first name is not given. As these two depictions represent the same person, I gave his full name as Benedict Harvest.

It is my sincere hope that by telling this story, I did right by those brave souls who fell upon the walls and in the hellish cauldron of the breaches. The Storming of Badajoz was deemed a British victory, as it opened the door for Wellington's army into Spain and set the stage for the eventual defeat of Napoleon. In the end, however, it was a terrible tragedy for all involved; the British, who went into the assault as valiant heroes, only to be driven mad by the horrors they faced. The equally brave French defenders who, had they surrendered, would have been damned to infamy as cowards, and yet whose valiant defence of the city led to so much needless suffering and death. And finally, to the Spanish citizens of Badajoz caught between two warring armies; neither those who corroborated with the French nor those who wished for liberation were spared the wrath of the redcoats' vengeance.

Like in all wars, there were no winners, only shattered survivors, many with broken bodies and tormented souls. The shadow of 6 April 1812 looms over Badajoz to this day. How many, then, must have wondered if their fallen comrades were the lucky ones after all?

*James Mace* – April 2012
200 Years after the Storming of Badajoz

Captain James Henry Webster returns in the epic novel of the Waterloo Campaign:

I Stood With Wellington

A Novel By

James Mace

# Further Reading

Cornwell, Bernard. *Sharpe's Company: Richard Sharpe and the Siege of Badajoz, January to April 1812.* London: HarperCollins, 2004.

Snow, Peter. *To War with Wellington: From the Peninsula to Waterloo.* London: John Murray Publishers, 2011.

# Illustration Credits

Cover: *The Storming of Badajoz*, by Chris Collingwood, copyright Cranston Fine Arts

Chapter I: *Arthur Wellesley, Duke of Wellington*, by Sir Thomas Lawrence, copyright English Heritage

Chapter II: *Marshal Nicolas Jean de Dieu Soult*, by George Peter Alexander Healy, copyright English Heritage

Chapter III: *Lieutenant General Sir Thomas Picton*, by Sir William Beechey, copyright English Heritage

Chapter IV: *Highlander with Spanish Militia*, artist unknown, taken from an ice pail given to the Duke of Wellington from the King of Prussia in 1819, copyright English Heritage

Chapter V: *English and Spanish Soldiers*, artist unknown, taken from an ice pail given to the Duke of Wellington from the King of Prussia in 1819, copyright English Heritage

Chapter IX: Close-up from *The Storming of Badajoz*, by Chris Collingwood, copyright Cranston Fine Arts

Chapter X: *Field Marshal Lord James Somerset*, by Jan Willem Pieneman, copyright English Heritage

Epilogue: *British Foot Guards*, artist unknown, taken from a wine cooler given to the Duke of Wellington from the King of Prussia in 1819, copyright English Heritage


For more information, please visit
http://www.englishheritageimages.com and
http://www.cranstonfinearts.com

CPSIA information can be obtained at www.ICGtesting.com
Printed in the USA
LVOW06s1743050614

388781LV00004B/921/P